12

Th

Throne

A Paranormal Romance
Royal Blood Book 1
by AJ Tipton

2015

"The Vampire's Throne"

By AJ Tipton

This is a work of fiction. All characters, names, places and incidents appearing in this work are fictitious. Any resemblance to real persons, living or dead, organizations, events or locales is purely coincidental.

All sexually active characters in this work are 18 years of age or older.

Cover art by CirceCorp

Alice Jones stifled a gag as she entered the perfume-saturated air of the high-end art gallery. Everything about the daunting gallery's decor was first-class rough chic, from the staggering large rooms with artistically exposed pipes in the ceiling to the intimate nooks of brick and glass.

Alice's borrowed stilettos threatened to dump her on her ass with every step, but she was determined to keep her head up. *Classy. Remember you're supposed to be classy,* she thought. With each nervous step, Alice half-expected someone to shout "plebeian intruder!" in her direction and tear her photographs off the wall. But, so far, the wealthy guests were nodding at her work politely and smiling as widely as their Botox allowed.

A heavy glass of wine materialized in her hand, and Alice looked up into the flashing grin of the gallery's owner, Margot Dal.

"You looked like you needed a drink." Margot nodded towards the glass, which was filled so high Alice was sure a slight breeze would spill it down her front.

"To wear?" Alice asked. She made a show of carefully craning down to sip at the brimming drink without moving her hand, while still sending Margot a grateful smile. Alice had been working closely with

Margot over the last few weeks to prepare for the opening, but the tall, statuesque woman still intimidated the crap out of Alice.

"What can I say? A good friend pushes your boundaries." Margot seemed to only be paying half attention to what she was saying, her eyes already roaming the crowd like she was looking for someone.

Alice forced herself not to fidget. She'd give anything for even *half* of Margot's composure. Margot looked effortlessly comfortable wherever she was, but within her gallery she was striking. Her dark skin glowed golden in the light, and her black dress was simple, tasteful, and probably cost more than twice Alice's rent. For her photographs' first big debut, Alice had scraped together every spare penny to get a new dress. She caught her own reflection and frowned. Her red hair was coming undone from her tightly-wound braid, sending out stray tendrils, and her bright blue eyes looked unnaturally wide between the thick lines of eye makeup. The strapless green dress wasn't too bad. It hugged her body, emphasizing the curve of her waist, with elaborate white beading along the top drawing the eye to her peeking cleavage. A purple shawl covered her shoulders and across her neck, the same color as her chandelier-beaded earrings. She resisted the urge to hide herself in the folds of her shawl. The longer she was here, the more she wished she'd taken up Margot's offer to borrow one of her many designer gowns.

"So, do you know if there have been any sales yet?" Alice sipped her drink cautiously, keeping her voice casual like she didn't particularly care about the answer.

Margot chuckled, not fooled at all. "Don't you worry, sweetie. Little red dots indicating finalized sales are going up all over the place." She raised her eyebrows at Alice. "But you know what would help those sales?"

"What?" Alice's stomach sank. She already knew what Margot was going to say.

"You need to *talk* to people. Help them get to know you, the stories behind your work." Margot flicked her wrist, the small gesture taking in the rest of the people in the gallery. "You know these rich folks; it's not just the art they want, it's the *secrets* behind the art." Margot gave Alice a stern look. "Sip down at least an inch of that wine and then shoo from this corner before I prod you out with a broom." Her tone was joking, but Alice had no doubt Margot would actually do it.

A woman who looked like she'd stepped off the cover of a magazine walked by and winked at

Margot. The gallery owner grabbed a new glass of wine from a passing waiter and smiled.

"Duty calls." Margot licked her lips and then gave Alice's hand a squeeze. "You can do this. This is your big night! Enjoy it." And then she was gone. Alice blinked and Margot was already on the other side of the room, smiling wide and standing intimately close to the cover girl.

Alice stared down at her drink. A couple more sips and it would be at a manageable height for mingling. She contemplated hiding in the corner for another hour just to be contrary, but she knew Margot was right. This show was her big chance to make the connections and cash to launch her photography career and escape her crappy day job as an administrative assistant. She took a deep gulp of the wine.

No more paperwork.

No more endless commutes.

No more wedging in photo shoots during thirty-minute lunch breaks.

Talking to strangers was downright palatable if it meant she could quit her soul-sucking corporate job. Her hand tightened around the stem of her wine glass. A well-dressed couple Alice vaguely recognized from a reality TV show were staring at her. The woman played with the edge of her leopard-print jacket while the man kept fiddling with his phone.

"It's all so derivative and prosaic." The woman sniffed loudly. "Rhys will have a good laugh over Margot's descent from good taste. What's with all the..." The woman pointed at Alice's closest photo, a high-contrast image of the bolts on the side of a trashcan at dusk.

Alice fought to keep a blush from creeping up her face. The man looked up from his phone. "What's that, snookums?"

"The title of the show, *Detail Wonders*. What's *wondrous* about a stupid trash can?"

The man shrugged. "Some rock star just bought the one with the hairbrush for five figures. He said it was urban or something."

"*Humans*, am I right? Such bullshit." She rubbed her nose, mumbling something about having to go to the bathroom, and the man nodded and followed.

Alice fought the urge to bury herself deeper into the corner. *Bullshit?* Getting the perfect photo required understanding the precise angle of the light, or catching the exact moment when the sun hit the--

Alice shook her head.

You can do this. You don't need their respect or their understanding. Someone just bought one of my photos for five figures! They can't all be shallow jerks. Just step up.

She managed to push forward one foot, then the next, until momentum pulled the rest of her toward the center of the room.

No day job.

No day job.

The words were a steady chant in her head as she smiled and nodded her way around the room. The folks who recognized her from the program's bio called out a few generic congratulations about her first big show. It was all very nice, but by the fiftieth time Alice told someone, "Yes, it's a real honor to be here," she worried her strain was starting to show.

Alice dabbed at the sweat behind her neck, looking around for Margot. *Will she skin me if I just pretend to have a headache and leave?* Alice wondered.

"I didn't think it could be possible for the artist to be more beautiful than the artwork," a smooth voice said from behind her.

Alice whipped around. Her glass tilted in her hand and she watched in what felt like slow motion as wine flew out of her glass in an arc toward a tall man with a trim beard standing a few feet away. The wine sprayed across him like a murder scene.

Noooooo. She reached out a hand like she could grab the liquid back from the air, but it was too late. The stain was already seeping through his crisp, white shirt like a blobby map of Asia across his chest.

"Oh my god! I'm so sorry!" Alice cried, jumping forward to dab the end of her shawl on the stain.

"It's quite all right." The man's voice was low and musical, sending little shivers down her spine. "This shirt needed a splash of color anyway."

Alice snuck a glance at his face, and his smile beamed at her like she was caught in a spotlight. She wanted to photograph his face from every angle. The Golden Ratio perfection of his features, the scruff of beard along the slope of his chin, the slight laugh lines around his mouth, and the care furrows on his forehead all demanded a zoom-in lens and the brightest light she could muster. She'd never been much for taking portraits, but this man--with the smile growing wider the longer she stared at him--was one she wanted to make into an intense study. *Preferably nude.*

"Um, hi. I'm Alice, and, uh, I take photos." Her words rushed out in a semi-incoherent string. She took a slow breath, forced herself to straighten up and stop staring at the sculpted muscles she could see through his wet shirt. "I'm usually more eloquent, I swear."

He laughed. "I believe it. Margot told me a lot about you; she's an old friend." He held out a hand. "Christopher Dal."

"Christopher Dal?" Alice shook his hand, feeling callouses along his palm that she didn't expect from somebody in a bespoke suit. "You and Margot have the same last name. Are you related?" They didn't look at all alike, but families came in all shapes and sizes.

He smiled. "No relation, but we've known each other so long she feels like family."

Alice felt a brief pang. She'd left behind all her hometown friends when she moved to the big city and had lost touch with everyone over the years. Between her job and her art, it was hard to find the time to make new friends. The warmth and familiarity in Christopher's voice when he said Margot's name sent a spike of loneliness through her. She forced a smile.

Christopher pointed at the picture behind her. "Your photos are remarkable."

"Thanks." She moved a wild strand of hair behind her ear, shifting her weight from one foot to the other.

"No, I mean it." Christopher stepped a little closer. "They're extraordinary. The way you honed in on such tiny details within mundane objects to find the hidden beauty is amazing. You have a remarkable eye."

Alice's repeated, "Thanks" was much more sincere this time. A happy warmth suffused her chest, flowing outward. *Finally!*

"Of all the people I've talked to tonight, you're the first one to understand that," Alice said. "I really appreciate it. I wanted people to walk away from this show with a new appreciation for the small details all around us."

Christopher smiled. "Isn't it fascinating how art can do that? It can present something that we look at every day in a different light to put the object into a new context."

Alice wanted to hug him. "That's exactly what I think! Beauty isn't just a sunset over the mountains." Her words picked up speed as she warmed to her topic. "Beauty can be the rim of a mailbox and how it complements the home behind it, or the construction of an anthill."

Christopher touched her hand and she felt the coolness of his skin like a soothing balm all the way down her arm. "You're an amazing artist, Alice. Do you realize how rare it is that you can see that, and then capture it so that others can see it too? You should be doing this full time."

Alice blushed. "You're being kind. I wish I had more time to really embrace my art." She pointed to a red dot next to the photo of a split tree. "I'm hoping the sales from tonight can help with that. I was lucky the light happened to be right a few minutes after I found that tree, but I almost missed it because of a meeting at work that ran late. There's never enough time to find every beautiful moment that's out there, but I'd sure like the chance to try."

Alice glanced accusingly at her wine, surprised she'd shared so much with a total stranger. From his small nods and understanding expression, Christopher seemed to know exactly what she meant.

"The world is so big," she said, "I wish I had the time to capture everything."

Christopher's grin broadened. "You never know. From what I've seen, tonight has been even more successful than even Margot anticipated." He held out his arm. "I've kept you too long from the rest of your guests. Do you feel like braving them together?"

Alice nodded, looping her arm through his and feeling the cords of muscles through his coat. Perhaps talking with strangers wasn't so bad, after all.

Christopher breathed in Alice's scent, intoxicating in its beauty: soap, a light touch of a vanilla perfume, and her blood pumping through the delicate skin of her neck. Suggestions of her mood sang from her blood: hesitation, anxiety, and...he really hoped he was interpreting it right...*longing*. Longing for him? Or just longing for a successful show? He would have to drink her blood to know for sure, and he was enjoying his time with her far too much to break the mood. As far as he could tell, she didn't have the Sight to recognize him as a vampire, or any of the other supernatural beings drinking wine and sniffing each other at the show.

His pulse raced at the gentle touch of Alice's hand against his forearm as they meandered through the gallery. Everything about her fascinated him. Her movements held a grace that hearkened back to refined royalty of centuries past, while her gentle spirit was like that of a magical, woodland nymph.

Her beauty shone like a beacon among the stilted bourgeois milling about the art gallery. As they walked arm and arm through the gallery, Alice's brilliant glow drew everyone they passed. Christopher settled into the role of the strong and silent companion, only jumping into the conversation to support Alice's lively explanation of her work. A tiger shifter flanked by her lovers came up to compliment a photo, and Alice launched into a charming, although somewhat rambling, description of why she photographed the cabinet in just that way. The tigress smiled, showing rows of perfect teeth, and Christopher felt himself stiffening up, protective instincts roaring to the surface which he clamped down before Alice noticed.

"I'm glad we dove back in." Alice's voice was steadier after the first lap around the room, but her grip on his arm was still tight with nerves.

"As am I." Christopher stared deeply into her bright, blue eyes.

I want to look into her eyes forever.

The thought flashed through him, stunning him with its certainty. He didn't sire other vampires often, but he always knew who he wanted within the first moments of meeting them. He pushed the thought down.

Not her. Please not her.

"Have you seen the rest of the exhibit?" He asked, actively distracting himself from his own thoughts.

Alice fiddled with the fringe on her wine-stained shawl. "I've seen it, but I'll be happy to view it again." She smiled at him. "There's so many wonderful pieces." Her joy was infectious and he held her hand against his arm, covering the back of her hand with his palm. Her skin was warm, her pulse beating fast as they moved into one of the side galleries of the other showcased artists.

She stopped short a little way into the room, pulling him with her.

"This one's my favorite," she said.

The photographer had captured the instant a champagne flute shattered. Glass shards flew in all directions, sparkling against a jet black background, forming perfectly symmetrical outlines like wings surrounding the remains of the glass.

"Absolutely stunning," Christopher said, not taking his eyes off of Alice.

A pink blush overtook Alice's cheeks. "You're not even looking at the art."

"Aren't I?" Christopher asked.

Alice blushed, turning quickly back towards the photograph. "Don't you just love this? An instant, captured forever. Something we'd never truly be able to appreciate if it wasn't frozen in time for us to see."

Christopher regarded the photo. "Being frozen in time is not all it is cracked up to be." He frowned.

"But, don't you see? Even if the image is frozen, what the viewer perceives isn't." Alice's entire face lit up. "It doesn't change over time, but time changes *it*." She pointed at the glass's stem in the picture. "You and I see a champagne flute, but in years to come, glass may be out of use and unrecognizable to people. Wouldn't that be magical? Seeing glass shatter for the first time, capturing what's a mundane moment for us in a way that translates across time?"

She'd make an amazing vampire. The tantalizing thought penetrated him again. "I see why Margot insisted you participate in this show. You have a unique perspective. Grounded, yet passionate," Christopher said.

"It's not usually an asset." Alice guided Christopher into a leisurely lap back to the main gallery. "I can't tell you how many school assignments I flunked because I got too carried away with the specifics."

He chuckled, noticing with a start that the art gallery had mostly emptied out, with only a few stragglers left. The gallery would be closing soon, and she would disappear from his life.

I should let her go. She would continue on her natural course: age and change and love and die like everybody else. And perhaps in a few hundred years he might forget the way light danced off of the curls of her hair, and how even the edge of a trashcan was lovely in her eyes.

"Would you mind if I call you sometime?" The words slipped out before Christopher could stop them, and yet he felt selfishly grateful they were out there. "I have had such an enchanting evening with you. I would love to continue our conversation."

Alice smiled, handing him a small, white card from her handbag. "I would love that. The 'business number' on there is my cell." She played with the edge of her shawl. "I had these made up for the show and thought it would look more professional."

"I'm sorry I completely monopolized you tonight." He didn't feel in the least bit sorry. "I hope you still had a good time."

Alice laughed. "Don't worry, I mingled as much as I could stand. You saved me from hiding in the corner all night. Besides..." She directed her gaze at her feet. "I enjoyed being monopolized." She rose onto her toes to give him a quick kiss on the cheek before hastily gathering her things and heading out the gallery door.

Christopher touched his face, the shadow of her kiss on his skin like a blazing brand. The last patrons stumbled together out the door, giggling into their last complimentary glass of wine, and then he was alone in the echoing room.

"Well done, Christopher." He hadn't heard Margot approach, but she could be as silent as a cat when she wanted to. She stood in front of one of Alice's photos which captured a small portion of a building's facade. The five-foot tall print showcased the intricate designs painstakingly crafted in a section of the cement.

"Alice told me this photo was taken seventy-two stories up. Can you believe it?" Margot asked. "She had to bribe a window washer to let her use his rig, but she didn't have the right harness. The wind at that height was so wild and strong, it nearly blew her off the side. It was a hell of a risk to take, but look at what she did with it." Margot sipped her glass of champagne thoughtfully, rising an eyebrow in his direction. "That kind of persistence, over centuries... I think we'd all be *very* impressed with what she could do."

Damn it, not Margot too. "Oh, hush," Christopher said. "That's not why I was talking to her, she's special and..." His voice trailed off when he looked over at Margot.

She was opening and closing her mouth like she was trying to speak, but no words came out. With an annoyed grimace, Margot pointed at her throat and then at Christopher.

Christopher's stomach churned. "Shit! I do *not* compel you to hush." His words reversed the compulsion of his inadvertent sire command, and Margot massaged her now unlocked jaw.

"Ugh. I'll never get used to that damn *hortari.*" Margot took an impressively-large swig out of the champagne glass she was holding.

"Me neither." Christopher sighed, running his fingers roughly through his hair. *This* was why he didn't see Margot or his other sirelings as often as he wanted. He'd gotten out of the habit of carefully choosing his words to avoid even the hint of a command. As the vampire who turned Margot from human to vampire-kind, his words were impossible for her to resist and he *hated* it. The sire command, called a *hortari,* was the one part of being a vampire that Christopher deeply resented.

This is why you cannot turn Alice, the rational voice in his mind reminded the part of him that still wanted to run after her.

He followed Margot back to a door marked "Staff Only" at the back of the gallery. She glanced at him and finished off her champagne like a shot.

"I'm sorry," he said.

She waved away his words, pressing a code into a keypad by the door. "Just watch it with the definitive sentences, okay?" She set down her glass. "I'm glad you were able to come tonight." The door slid open and the lights switched on to reveal a high-ceilinged room. Art covered every inch of the walls and up onto the ceiling, most of it hundreds of years old: masks from Nigeria and Mali, paintings from Parisian masters who never got their big breaks, headdresses from Native American cultures so old that their names were lost to time. The effect was chaotic and a little mad, but still gorgeous, much like the room's decorator. Christopher never regretted giving Margot the chance at immortality, and she'd used her time well.

"Tell me, how have you been?" He asked.

Margot poured another glass of champagne. "Fine as things go. Roxanne the succubus passed through town a few weeks ago and we had some fun before she moved on." Margot waved the bottle in his direction. "Want any of this?"

"No thanks. I never understood why you drink that human stuff. It's not like you're able to get drunk."

"I like the bubbles." Margot walked over to the wall and tilted a stunning portrait of a naked woman to the side until Christopher heard a *click*. "But you have the look of someone who needs to get drunk for real, and I have some excellent options in here." A panel in the wall opened up, revealing a bar set and wine fridge filled with hanging bags of blood.

"Anything 'A positive' would be great, thanks." Christopher stretched his arms behind his back and sat down on one of the low couches in the middle of the room.

Margot handed him a crystal glass filled with blood. "Cheers." She sipped deeply from her own glass. "I have an instinct about you and Alice."

Christopher sat up straight, nearly spilling the blood down his wine-sprayed shirt. "What are you talking about?"

She laughed. "You, her, the way you just jumped at the sound of her name like you got poked by a unicorn in the ass." She swirled the blood in her glass slightly. "I'm not wrong. You like her."

He leaned back. "She's magnificent, what's not to like?" Christopher sipped from his own glass. Emotions from the blood's donor washed over him as the crimson liquid necessary for his survival coursed down his throat. The male donor had been drunk and in love when he donated, his emotions rich and rolling within his blood. With each sip of the man's heady happiness, Christopher wondered more about what Alice was doing right now. He eyed his glass, then Margot. With her choice of vintage, she was definitely trying to play matchmaker.

"Alice has a profoundly passionate worldview and a good eye." Margot pointed an accusatory finger at Christopher. "Perception like that is worth preserving for the centuries."

He groaned. Margot's words matched so closely how he'd felt when he first met Alice.

"That's true." Christopher took a long gulp of blood. "The way she thinks, her passion, her kindness..." He turned away. "...her immense beauty. It would be a crime to let all she is wither and fade away."

Margot frowned. "Then why are you hesitating?"

"I'm not." He was. "If she agrees to be turned, I *will* do it, but..."

"But you have your *rules*," Margot smiled, her expression wicked. "You must want her *bad* if you're this conflicted about turning her. Poor sire. You can bang her, *or* turn her." Margot kicked off her high heels with a happy sigh, settling next to him on the couch.

"You know why I have my rules. It would be monstrous to sleep with somebody I have such *absolute* control over." Christopher sighed. "I can barely spend time with you or the rest of my sirelings as it is. But you're right, I need to put my attraction to her aside." He nodded, sure in his decision. "She'll be a tremendous asset to my sire line, to our family."

"Good. I'll be glad to have her. You're a good sire. Even if we're sad we don't get to see you often, we're all grateful you're so careful with avoiding the sire compulsion."

Christopher shrugged. His brother, Rhys, had a distinctly different view of how a sire should treat his turned vamps. In his twisted way, he thought he was actually *helping* his sirelings by taking away their will. As the last sirelings of the Vampire King, Christopher and Rhys were the only heirs, and their conflicting approaches to sireing made presenting a unified example for their people impossible. Christopher had spent centuries trying to convince the king to set laws for how sirelings should be treated, with no success.

"I'll offer Alice the transition, explain how it all works, and let her decide." Christopher said.

"I'll drink to that." Margot lifted her glass.

"To Alice."

Alice rechecked her phone to confirm she had come to the right place. When Christopher texted her where they were going to meet, she hadn't been sure what to expect, but a smoky dive bar with a pink, neon sign reading "AUDREY'S", was not what she had pictured. AUDREY'S was a lone building several stories tall surrounded by dark forest, with a parking lot mostly filled with motorcycles and beat-up sedans. Frost on the front windows made it difficult to see much inside, but Alice liked the feel of the place. Music curled out of the entrance's double doors, with laughter and light creating the welcoming glow of a lighthouse's beacon.

Her phone beeped with a text from Christopher confirming that he'd arrived and was waiting for her at the bar. He must have arrived right before she did. *Punctual and polite. Two more points for the hot guy.* She smiled. After her last few disappointing dates, tonight was looking very promising.

Alice stepped through the doors and was immediately hit with the strongest allergic reaction she'd ever had. Her vision misted, her eyes itched, and her headache felt like something large was pounding to escape her forehead. She pressed her fingers to the bridge of her nose and held her breath, hoping the feeling would pass.

Crap. Not now. She'd had this kind of allergy attack before, but it usually only lasted a couple of seconds. She was hiking the last time this happened. Her headache flared up just as she'd passed a group of folks watching a track and field event. It was only after she'd climbed a ways away and stopped even *thinking* about what she'd seen that the feeling cleared.

Through what felt like a cloudy film over her eyes, Alice scanned the crowd around the bar for Christopher. She found him in intense discussion with the bartender, a pale woman with a mane of black braids sticking up from her head and an intricate rose tattoo that took up most of her chest.

Christopher looked so gorgeous Alice had to stop and collect herself. He filled out his jeans, sneakers, and t-shirt so perfectly, it was like they were tailored to show off the tapered lines of his waist, the curve of his shoulders, and the tight cording of his biceps. His hands were clenched so tightly around his glass, the skin on his fingers was almost white, and his eyebrows were furrowed with stress. The bartender kept mixing and handing out drinks to other patrons, but her expression of patient compassion didn't waver from Christopher's face. Neither seemed to have noticed Alice yet as she made her way carefully through the crowd, her headache getting worse the further she waded into the bar.

To her left, four big guys with mohawks were grunting loudly as they egged on a furious arm wrestling competition taking place at the next table between a petite, teenage girl in a floral dress and a looming beast of a man with skin so pale, he looked almost blue. Alice blinked, her headache spiking as she looked at them, and for a second it almost appeared like the men with mohawks had green skin and the teenager had flowers growing out of her hair. Alice shook her head. *That's impossible.* Alice's headache faded for a second and the flower woman was once more just a girl, the men were biker dudes, and the big guy was just being nice by pretending to strain against the girl's strength.

A bird flew across the rafters, nearly hitting Alice in the face and she let out a small squeal of alarm. *What's a bird doing in here?*

A hand gently cradled her elbow, and Alice recognized the callouses against her skin even before she turned to confirm Christopher had found her. His skin felt even colder than she remembered from the gallery, but it was strangely soothing in contrast to the hot roar of her headache.

Christopher smiled at her. "I'm glad you made it. Sorry, this place can be a bit much."

Alice didn't mind leaning on him a bit for balance as they made their way over to the bar. "It's okay. I think someone must be wearing a perfume or something that's aggravating my allergies. I was hoping you wouldn't mind if we went someplace else?"

Christopher shared a glance with the bartender. The woman leaned over the bar, stretching out a hand to Alice.

"Hi, I'm Lola. It's been a while since we had some fresh blood in here." Lola smiled, flashing white teeth. "That headache is your perception of reality getting threatened, and your body trying to fight it off. Ignore everything except me and Christopher and you'll feel a lot better."

What the hell? My perception of reality? Alice shook the bartender's hand automatically and her headache disappeared like turning off a light.

Alice sunk onto one of the padded barstools. The misty feeling still hung over her eyes and Alice tried to blink it away. *What's happening?* A sensible, quiet voice inside her head was screaming at her to run away from this place as quickly as possible, but she was too curious to leave. She glanced at Christopher. He was looking at her with an expression of hope that warmed her down to her toes.

Christopher's handsomeness was almost unreal in its perfection. His features were perfectly symmetrical, the only imperfection a tiny scar along one cheek above the line of his beard, and his tousled hair which seemed to fly in whatever direction it wanted. The bartender slid a pink drink across the bar and Alice grabbed it before it slid off the ledge.

"Good save." Lola winked and turned away to serve something bright green to a stocky man whose head barely reached the top of the counter.

Alice flinched as the bird flew past, barely missing her head. It landed on the shoulder of the young girl who was still arm wrestling.

"That poor bird." Alice blinked rapidly. The whole room looked like it was swimming behind a misty veil. "We should try to help it out of here, shouldn't we? I bet that bartender has something we could use."

Christopher settled on the stool next to Alice, looking at her with concern in his deep, brown eyes.

"That's not a bird. We can still go if you want. If we continue to stay here, I suspect your worldview is going to be changed forever. I know of another place where we could go if you're not up for that."

Alice took a sip of the drink. It tasted divine, with an initial sweetness which gave way to a spicy aftertaste that nipped at the back of her throat all the way down. Alice shook her head. All this talk of challenging reality was a little weird, but she wasn't leaving the best cocktail she'd had in years.

"It's okay. I like it here. It's just not where I would have pictured our first date."

Christopher leaned back from her quickly, all trace of humor erased from his face. "Ms. Jones, I invited you here because there's a business arrangement I would like to discuss with you.

Alice felt a blush surge up into her cheeks. *I'm such an idiot! Of course, this isn't a date.* "Oh, right. I hadn't realized." She frantically scrambled for a shred of dignity. "What an interesting venue for a business meeting. What can I do for you?"

"I invited you here because I think the world would be a better place if you continued to live in it beyond your natural lifespan." Christopher's tone was serious.

"What?" Her headache was brewing again behind her temple.

"I'm a vampire. And I think you would make a great vampire too."

The headache was back in full force, building like a wave of heat. She took a long gulp of her drink, but all she could taste now was the burn. Alice peered at Christopher, waiting for him to smile and admit that it was all just a big joke.

"Vampires don't exist." *Of course I end up on a non-date with a crazy person.* "You're certainly welcome to believe in whatever you want, but I think I'll be going now," she said slowly.

Christopher reached forward to gently lay his hand on top of hers on the bar. "Wait just a moment. Look around. Look *closer*. Most humans ignore the supernatural with a stubbornness that lasts a lifetime, but you're an artist. You've been discovering beauty your whole life." His fingers rubbed along the top of her hand, sending little shivers of want up her arm. *Why is it the hot ones are always unhinged?* She shifted in her chair, trying to ignore what he was saying, but the misty feeling in front of her eyes was *fading* like an opaque veil becoming more transparent by the moment.

How is this possible? There was no denying that something was definitely happening.

Christopher's voice dropped to a low hum, sexy and strong. "It's up to you. You can go back to your old life. You can forget all of this, write me off as some nut you met at a gallery. But you have to decide."

"Decide what?" The headache pounded like a desert rave. What had Lola said? That the headache was the challenge to her perception? If Alice wanted it to stop, she knew what she had to do: focus on the grains of wood on the bar, look at her glass, look at what was sane.

Maybe it's time for a little crazy. She remembered at the art gallery, shyly tucking herself away. If she hadn't taken a risk, she would never have met Christopher, wouldn't be here now. If there was something *more* to the world which she hadn't been able to see, didn't she owe it to herself to find the truth? Even if everything about this was utterly insane.

She straightened in her chair and looked out into the room, concentrating on every detail she could spot.

"That's it." She could hear the smile in Christopher's voice, even though she wasn't looking at him. "See the truth. There are more wonders in the world than we could see in twenty lifetimes."

She clutched his hand like a lifeline. The misty look of the room shimmered, and then ripped apart like a curtain tearing at the seams. Every memory when she'd thought she was having an allergic reaction flooded in all at once, with new vision.

Months ago she'd looked up to see low-flying airplanes and gotten a massive headache. *Those weren't planes.* They'd been brightly-scaled dragons flying together across the sky. The track and field event she'd seen had been an elaborate obstacle course of men and women transforming back and forth between animal and human forms as they overcame magical barriers.

"Ms. Jones?" Christopher gave her shoulder a little shake.

Alice blinked, frozen by fear and awe fighting each other under her skin. *Everything I know about the world is wrong.*

"Alice, are you okay?"

At the table less than ten feet away, the men with the mohawks looked like trolls from storybooks, their skin swamp green and their brightly-colored hair actually rocks sprouting from the top of their heads. A blue-skinned man with marble-white skin and hands like claws was arm wrestling with all his might against a woman with golden skin, flowers sprouting from her forehead, and rainbow wings fluttering from her back. On her shoulder sat a tiny brown-skinned man riding an oversized butterfly, a bow and arrow strapped to his shoulders.

"Alice?" Christopher's voice had been calling to her for the last minute, but she'd barely heard.

"There's so much." Her voice sounded like it was coming from far away.

Dragons, magic, vampires, *everything* was real.

"It's a lot," Christopher said. "Are you okay?"

Alice nodded. "I never knew the world was so..." She waved vaguely at the woman with wings. "That there are so many *amazing* things all around us. Will I always be able to see things this way?"

Christopher nodded. "Yes. Once you see this world, you can almost never un-see it. If you were really determined, you could probably convince yourself that this was just a dream, but if you want to continue seeing the truth, you'll see it forever."

A roar went up from behind them. The woman--"a pixie," Christopher whispered in her ear, his breath brushing against her neck spreading goosebumps down her back--had defeated the blue-skinned man in the arm wrestling contest. The pixie jumped up on the table, sending the tiny man riding the butterfly on her shoulder rocketing up into the air.

"Suck it, yeti boy!" the pixie squeaked in a high-pitched voice. "Suck it, everyone!" She threw up both middle fingers, and the yeti laughed. He scooped her up off the table and deposited her into his lap, where they started making out with loud slurping noises and groans. Everyone in the bar clapped and cheered, and Alice found herself clapping along.

"Let's get some air," Christopher said, holding out his arm for her.

She grabbed hold, appreciating Christopher's help dismounting her bar stool. She turned to pay her tab, but Lola waved her off.

"Come back here after you and Chris have your talk." Lola smiled. "Good luck."

Alice nodded, smiling her thanks as she followed Christopher out the back door to the wide field behind the bar. The field was littered with a series of hay bales and low hurdles like at a horse riding competition. The sound of traffic from the street was almost a whisper, and the low murmur of voices from the bar and the roar of the wind through the trees were the only sounds Alice could hear in the still night.

The moon was bright and beamed down, highlighting Christopher's face into stark contrasts of black and white. He grinned and walked forward, effortlessly hopping onto the top of a ten-foot stack of bales; it was so high his feet swung level with Alice's head. He spread his hands out wide like a magician completing a trick and grinned. Alice noticed for the first time his front canines were two sharp points. A shiver ran down her spine.

Vampire.

He hadn't been lying. The ramifications struck her like a train.

Christopher Dal really is a vampire.

She'd spilled her wine on a vampire the first time she saw him.

She'd given her number to a vampire.

"This is crazy," she said, her voice barely louder than a whisper.

Christopher jumped down, landing effortlessly with barely a sound. "I know. Not everybody can handle the truth the way I believe you can. The fact that you're not running away is further evidence that I am right about you." He stepped closer. The scent from his body was woody with a slight musk, and it made her long to snuggle up against him and lick along his neck.

This isn't a date, he'd said.

It was hard for Alice to remember why he'd invited her here. With Christopher standing so close, the fabric of her dress brushed against his t-shirt when she breathed in and out. He leaned down and, for a second, she was sure he was going to kiss her. His fingertips caressed along her shoulders, brushing against a few tendrils of red hair which had come loose from her braid.

"You have the flexibility of mind to be a great vampire," he said. "And, believe me, the condition comes with some major advantages."

That's right! He wants me to be a vampire!

Alice stepped back from him, distancing herself from the intoxication of his scent and the temptation of rubbing her cheek against the scruff of his beard. In the days since her photographs were displayed at Margot's gallery, she'd barely gotten her head around the idea that she might actually be able to leave her crappy job and be a full time photographer. But becoming a vampire? That was a life change beyond her wildest dreams.

"Immortality is just the beginning," Christopher continued. He leaned back against the hay bale and crossed his arms like a chiseled model at a cover shoot. "You'll be able to smell emotions. With other vampires, they'd have to be cut and their blood exposed to the air, or you'll have to drink it directly, but with non-vampires, you can sense their feelings through their skin just by being close to them." He nodded to her. "Like right now, I can smell your amazement, and a tinge of fear at what I'm offering you."

Alice blushed scarlet. He could smell her emotions?

Christopher smiled. "You don't have to be embarrassed."

He stepped forward and she instinctively pressed closer. He cupped her face between his hands and leaned down until his breath brushed across her lips.

"That desire you feel?" He was so close. The strength of him, the power of him, was a pull stronger than she'd ever felt before. A thrill shot down spine, pooling in wetness between her legs. "I feel it too." His voice was like a purr. "You're so beautiful, I can barely stand it."

Kiss me! Kiss me! Alice hoped her blood was screaming it to him as strongly as she screamed in her own head. She reached forward to grab his waist, but he released her, withdrawing fast like her emotions burned him.

"But there's a few downsides to being a vampire." Christopher turned away, jumping back to the top of the hale bale, far from her. "The most important one is the sire compulsion. The vampire who turns you has absolute command over you. We call it *hortari*. The origin of the *hortari* was to protect the population from the strength and hunger of newly-turned vampires. A sire's will is binding no matter what the command, even if the sire didn't mean to issue a command."

"I would have to do whatever you tell me?"

Christopher nodded. "It's not a power to be taken lightly. You'll have supernatural strength, speed, and live forever, looking exactly as you are now, unless someone takes off your head or sets you on fire. You'll only receive nourishment from blood, although you can still enjoy the taste of food and drink. And knowing the emotional states of those around you is helpful in more situations than you'd think."

Alice felt lightheaded with all of the possibilities. *Am I really considering becoming a vampire?*

Christopher stood up on the top of the hay bale and flipped through the air in a tight somersault to land on tip-toe on the top of the narrow wall ten feet from him. Her heart leapt into her throat, sure he was going to break his neck before she remembered, *Right. Vampire.* He made another jump, this time landing on his hands and flipping back upright a few yards away with a smooth grace that would put the most experienced acrobat to shame.

That could be me.

The thought was more tempting than she'd anticipated. She'd live forever without aging. Forever with Christopher. She'd never felt so attuned to a man before, his kindness and attention at the gallery like a scene from her dearest dreams. The memory of his breath on her lips, the brush of his chest against her dress, teasing her breasts with that brief flutter of contact, sent new shivers of want coursing through her body. What would sex be like as a vampire? With all that strength and speed, it had to be super intense. If she drank Christopher's blood while they were making love, she'd be able to feel everything he was feeling, enjoy the pleasure she was giving him. She swallowed to keep from drooling.

"Alice." Christopher's voice had an edge. "Your longing is calling to me. You must know, if I'm going to sire you, we can never be together. Not like that."

His words splashed against her skin like a burst of cold water.

What?

"The sire compulsion is too strong. I could never make love to you knowing that if I phrased my words in the wrong way, you would lose your free will to choose."

"But, I *want* to be with you..."

He shook his head. "I take my responsibility as a sire seriously. Once I sire you, no matter how we might feel for each other, we would have to go our separate ways. My other sirelings would be your mentors to guide you through this life without robbing you of your agency. They're good people. I chose them the same way I chose you: I knew that they could make the world a better place if they had more time."

"But--"

Christopher stepped farther away from her. "There's a lot for you to think about. You know how to contact me when you have your answer. Take your time." He winked at her. "We have all the time in the world."

He turned away and disappeared around the corner of the bar before Alice could put the puzzle of her thoughts into something resembling a complete picture. *Vampires are real. Dragons, pixies, what else was real out there? Witches? Werewolves? Ghosts?* All those magical creatures were really out there. *I could be one.* She pressed her fingers against her forehead. *I have time to decide.*

Remembering that she still had to pay for her tab at the bar, Alice walked back into AUDREY's feeling like she was still half in a dream.

The sense of unreality strengthened when she arrived inside. The pixie and yeti had gone off to finish off their evening and the four trolls were singing a drinking song that was off-key, didn't rhyme, and seemed to have four different tunes at once.

At the bar, with her legs crossed to reveal an impressive amount of skin through a slit in her red dress, perched Margot Dal. The gallery owner raised a flute of champagne in Alice's direction and patted the empty stool next to her.

"Hey, hon. I heard Christopher gave you the pitch," Margot said. She smiled, revealing pointed canines.

"Holy shit, you're a..." Alice swallowed the word before she said it.

Margot licked her lips. "Yep, I'm a vampire. Actually, I'm Christopher's first sireling. He turned me centuries ago, back when being black, a woman, and a lesbian was immediately worthy of capital punishment." She wrinkled her nose. "The world is...better now. Accepting an offer of near-invincibility was an easy choice for me." Margot eyed Alice. "But you have other choices. And there are costs to being what I am."

"Christopher mentioned the *hortari* whatsit. Does Christopher... has he ever made you do anything?"

Margot shook her head. "Never on purpose. He's always been very careful, but it's ridiculously easy to slip up. He's a good sire that way; a lot of other vamps get off on the power to make sirelings dance to their tune. Christopher's brother, Rhys, is a piece of work that way. If you accept Christopher's offer, you'll definitely have to meet that ass-wipe, although you won't be compelled to obey him." She set down her glass. "I don't mean to throw all of this at you at once, but you should have all the details." She held up her hand and counted off the points on each finger. "Becoming a vampire means you'll never get pregnant, *but* you'll never have your period again so that's a win. You'll be able to eat all the food you want and never absorb any of it, so you'll never gain a pound. Picture eating fudge non-stop for the rest of eternity and still looking as delightfully trim as you are right now. The only thing you'll *need* to consume is blood."

Alice had never really thought about kids. She'd vaguely assumed it might happen eventually, but she'd never really pursued it. She'd always figured it was one of those things that just *happened* over time.

But I'd be able to see the world, explore all its beauties forever.

"You really drink blood?" Alice asked.

"Yeah, it takes some getting used to. Some old-school vamps drink directly from the neck, and during sex it's stupid fun, but mostly we have arrangements with blood banks where they give us the old bags that are no longer viable for humans."

"So, let's just say that I decide to become a vampire..." Alice said. It was surprisingly easy to consider once she'd wrapped her head around it. The sire compulsion was worrying, but if Christopher kept his word--and every instinct she had declared that he would--then he would stay away to allow her autonomy. Vampirism was a chance to have the *time* to accomplish everything she ever wanted. She would be an idiot to turn down this chance. But then...there was Christopher.

"Yes?" Margot sat forward, looking excited.

"Um, would *you* turn me? We're already friends and I trust you. And, uh, if Christopher's not my sire, then maybe..."

"Then he'd consider a relationship?" Margot chuckled at Alice's blush. "Sweetie, your hormones have been screaming at him since I pointed him in your direction at the gallery. But, sorry, I don't sire people. I'm happy to train other vamps' sirelings, and be a good friend to the rest of Christopher's sire line, but having my own sire line isn't something I've ever wanted. Sorry, hon, if you want all of this..." She gestured around at the hubbub of supernatural beings having fun around them. "Then Christopher's your best chance." Margot swung off of her bar stool. "It's all up to you." She pushed some cash across the bar at Lola. "I got your tab. Whatever you decide, definitely hit me up when you're ready for your next show."

Alice nodded, the gallery and her previous life feeling far away. At the end of the bar, a woman with bright red hair and horns coming out of her head cursed at the trolls to "shut the fuck up, or I will wish you into deep space!", and the trolls quieted down with minimal grumbles. A wolf was sleeping under one of the tables, a dish of what looked like beer cradled between his paws. Curled up against the wolf's back was an immense lioness who was chewing on the wolf's ear in a way that looked simultaneously intimate and annoying, but the wolf only grunted in his sleep and kicked his back legs.

"I want this," Alice said. She thought she said it too quietly for anyone to hear, but Lola's silky voice replied behind her,

"Then go get it."

Alice grinned and jumped off her stool. The future looked like it was going to be magical. She just had to find a way to keep Christopher in it.

Christopher sipped from his crystal glass of blood and leaned back against his long Chesterfield couch, the rounded back cushioning his head as he let out a long breath. He'd chosen blood donated by a yoga master to try and drink up a little calm, but it wasn't working.

He set his glass down before his grip threatened to shatter the antique and closed his eyes, willing himself to think about anything but Alice. Or the way the light hit her hair. Or the way the smell of her intense longing had so perfectly mirrored his own that it had taken centuries of self-control to not pull her to him and kiss her until her knees shook.

The world will benefit from her as a vampire, he told his cock, which was already half-hard at the mere memory of her. That growing part of him was hoping she'd turn down his offer, that she'd decide to stay human. It would mean only a few brief decades with her before he and the world lost that light in her eyes, but he'd be able to carry the memory of her touch, the feeling of her lips, with him through all the long years to come.

"It's her choice," he told his empty living room. He'd decorated his home in the 1920s during what Margot laughingly referred to as his Gatsby phase, and never bothered to change anything beyond the crucial updates for electricity, plumbing, and Wi-Fi. All the chairs and sofas were wide and cushioned, grand Oriental rugs covered bold black and white-checkered tiles, and paintings from forgotten masters took up most of the walls. Tiffany lamps blazed color along the Art Deco lines up the wall to the tall ceiling dripping with chandeliers.

Christopher picked up his glass, took a long gulp of the blood, and waited for the yogi's serenity to wash through him. He propped his slippered feet up on the couch and closed his eyes.

Rhys was growing bolder. Christopher's brother was beginning to make public claims that he was going to "clean up" the vampire community and "deal with dissenters", whatever that meant. Christopher had come home to a note scrawled on his fridge from his sireling, Danny, that Christopher's lieutenants-- the four vampires Christopher had turned directly--were going to be gathering the next day to discuss Rhys's hateful rhetoric and what they were going to do about it. It wasn't as if the king would ever do anything. Christopher took a long sip of blood. His sire's leadership style of using *hortari* on his sirelings when needed and then apathetic neglect the rest of the time meant Rhys could get away with *actual* murder so long as his actions didn't impact the king's immediate comfort. Christopher would just have to be careful. As the eldest of the king's turned, Christopher was his sire's heir apparent, but vampire tradition allowed for a challenge.

Perhaps now isn't the right time for siring a new vampire.

Christopher pushed down the selfish thought before he began to believe it. There was always trouble, in one form or another; if Alice wanted to become a vampire, his own wish for romance shouldn't hold her back.

The sound of his doorbell startled him so badly he spilled a splatter of blood down his shirt.

"Damn." He tried to brush it away, smearing the drops into gruesome finger painting across his chest.

The doorbell rang again and he called out, "Coming!" as he grabbed a jacket hanging by the door to hide the stains.

He checked the view-hole in the door, and his hand shook slightly as he opened the door.

"Alice," he said.

She looked amazing. Her eyes sparkled in the moonlight, and she'd changed into the green dress she'd worn at the gallery which hugged her lean curves. Excitement and fear came off of her skin in waves. He knew what she was going to say before she opened her mouth.

"I'm in. I want to be like you." As soon as she said the words, the smell of excitement in her blood spiked, and she shifted her weight to her toes like a little dance. She was so lovely it hurt.

A small, petty voice in his head reminded him that Alice's choice meant that she wanted to be a vampire more than she wanted to be with him. He pushed down the feeling.

"That's wonderful news! Come on in." Christopher stepped back to allow Alice inside, savoring the sweet scent of her as she walked by. The excitement rolling off her still warred with her fear, but under those, he could smell a thrilled arousal in Alice's blood that gave him pause.

"You have such a beautiful home!" Alice twirled in the foyer, a wide, circular room lined with alternating panels of cherrywood and floor-to-ceiling windows. The moonlight spilled in, bathing Alice in a warm glow. She pointed to the windows. "I thought daylight was a no-no for your kind." She stopped short. "Our kind?"

"Curtains." Christopher pressed a code into his cell phone and reams of dark fabric lowered over the windows. Without the moonlight, the space felt darker, more intimate.

"This I like even more." Alice's voice was low. She stepped forward, her fingertips tracing the lines of his jacket. The slight brush of her touch made him bite back a groan. Everything about her called to him. She was so close, he could feel the heat radiating off her body, hear the blood coursing through her veins, and smell her desire. He tensed up, balling his fists, desperately trying to stop himself from leaning forward and capturing her lips. He couldn't bring himself to move away, but he managed to not move any closer either.

She opened his jacket, her eyes widening at the splatter of blood across his shirt. She laughed, the sound so light and enchanting Christopher's fists clenched white.

"I'm glad I'm not the only one who has trouble keeping your shirt clean."

He laughed too, then cut himself off. *I'm toast, we already have inside jokes*. He shifted his weight so he stood infinitesimally closer and the beaded top of her dress brushed against his shirt.

"You know I can smell your emotions, Alice." Christopher spoke, regretting each word as he formed it. He reached up to brush a fingertip along her face, her skin smooth and perfect. "We cannot be together, not in that way."

"Actually," Alice reached up to hold his hand against her face, leaning her cheek into his palm. "You said we couldn't be together *after* I've been turned." She turned her head, placing a kiss on his skin that sent lines of fire down his arm and through his torso.

Yessss! Every cell in his body demanded.

Alice ran her other hand down his chest, her fingers tracing the pattern of red, making little circles. "Right now, I'm still human. And I want to have one, last, purely human experience before I'm changed forever. And I want it to be with you, Christopher."

Her blood smelled of a primal desire boiling deeper than just saying farewell to her humanity. Christopher couldn't resist running his hands through her hair, caressing the back of her neck and watching the goosebumps rise along the trail of his fingers. *This is such a bad idea.* He was already half in love with her. Knowing what it would be like to really be with her, and then denying himself her touch for the rest of eternity, would be excruciating. *Is a lifetime of pain worth it for just one night?*

"I can see you thinking it over, weighing the pros and cons." Alice smiled. "You may have vampire senses, but sometimes I can tell what *you're* thinking."

Alice stared up at him, questioning. She raised a hand to mirror his touch on her face, her nimble fingers tracing along the sharp edge of Christopher's jawline, then dancing down to the sensitive surface of his mouth, and teasing across his bottom lip. He groaned, biting down gently on her fingertips.

But-- He was a man at war with himself, and each side was losing.

Alice pushed onto her tiptoes to align her mouth with his. "Don't you want this?" She asked, before capturing his lips with her own.

All resistance, all composure fled Christopher's being as he responded to Alice's kiss, his passion flaring up to match hers. His hands roamed her body, discovering new territory, mapping the hills and valleys of her form.

"Gods, I want you so much," he groaned.

"Good, because if this is only going to be the one night..." Her voice hitched slightly. "Then we need to make it count."

Alice unbuttoned Christopher's shirt, her mouth following her hands in a sensuous trail down his torso. He leaned his head back, reveling in the sensations from her lips, her tongue, her teeth. She lightly traced her tongue along the grooves of his six-pack, pleasure tickling down along every nerve ending.

In a sudden movement, Alice loosened Christopher's belt and swept Christopher's pants and boxers to the ground. She raked her nails up his calves, winding her way up to where he needed her most.

"You don't need to do this." He was panting now, the sight of her sultry smile the most gorgeous thing he'd seen in five hundred years.

"Oh yes, I do." She licked her lips. "I'm going to bring you, my handsome vampire, to your knees."

He let out a groan of pleasure as she licked a line up his swollen shaft, teasing him with her mouth as her hands wound around to grasp his ass.

Her red hair spilled over her green dress in a sensuous wave, and he knew he wouldn't be able to resist unwrapping her for much longer. She looked up, and her shockingly blue eyes pierced him as she finally took him into her mouth. She moaned around his hard length, sending waves of pleasure through Christopher's body as he reveled in the feel of her lips and tongue dancing along his cock. He twined his fingers through her hair and watched, entranced, as she bobbed along his length.

Alice smiled as she released him with a pop, and Christopher struggled against his release. He wanted their first time together--their *only* time--to last.

Christopher pulled Alice to her feet, spinning her so her back was flat against his chest. He looked around the stark foyer. They'd barely moved four feet from the door since she arrived. He grabbed her under her knees and swung her up into his arms.

"We need the proper setting for this," he said.

She squealed and hugged his neck as he ran up the stairs two at a time, not caring about his crumpled pants lying in the middle of the foyer. The roaring desire in her veins smelled glorious.

"Christo--" He ran so fast, he kicked his bedroom door open and deposited Alice on the bed before she could finish the word. Her voice changed to a cooing, "ooo" when she saw the room. The ceiling was draped with hanging silk, the enormous four-poster bed piled high with pillows, and the crystal chandelier sparkled the light into rainbow prisms.

"This is amazing," she said, her hands still around his neck.

Christopher slid his hands around the contours of her dress, finding a single, long zipper that ran from her neck to her ass.

"*This* is far more so." With a low growl, he slowly unzipped her, following the zipper with a long trail of nips and kisses down her back. The dress slid easily off her body, and Christopher's arousal grew when he realized she wasn't wearing anything underneath her dress.

He stood back in awe of her. Her breasts were everything he'd dreamed they would be, round and pert, her nipples already pebbled in arousal, and the slight indentations of her muscled core lean and perfect.

Alice raised an eyebrow at him, her stance confident in her nudity, and kissed him gently on the lips. She stroked his erect cock, her touch feeling so good a drop of pre-cum beaded at his tip.

Christopher scooped Alice up with one arm, and deposited the giggling temptress onto the bed. He peppered the sensitive skin of her inner thighs with kisses, moving closer and closer to her core. Alice sighed happily and bucked her hips, every emotion he could smell off her skin begging him for more. His fingers played with the sensitive skin along her stomach and sides, stroking under her knees and along her arms.

"Don't be a tease." Alice's hands roamed her own body, grasping at the nipples of her exposed breasts.

"How can I not? You look so beautiful when I keep you waiting." Christopher winked.

Christopher's skilled tongue moved to Alice's soaked core, gently running laps around her sensitive flesh. He flicked the very tip of his tongue at her clit, and bit back a smile as she melted underneath him. He covered her mound with his mouth, sucking and kissing her as Alice moaned.

"Holy fuck, that feels good," Alice whimpered. "Christopher, I'm so close."

The scent of her arousal intoxicated him. The emotions flowing from her: excitement, trust, and something more, something deeper, called to him. Christopher latched onto Alice's clit with his mouth and pounded two fingers into her sopping core, moving inside her with a merciless rhythm. Alice shouted out in pleasure as she pulsed around his fingers. He kept moving inside of her until he felt a second orgasm rip through her body, and she shuddered around him once more. Her pleasure overwhelmed him until he felt like he was drowning in it.

Alice pulled Christopher onto the bed and he was helpless to resist. She pushed him onto his back and pulled off his shirt so he was naked before her. Her admiration of his hard muscles, well-defined pecs, and abs flowed off her in waves, her pulse increasing with the strong scent of anticipation.

He felt exposed for the first time, every want and dream for her, for them, laid bare. She licked her lips as she moved over him. Her hair was wild with red strands stuck with sweat to her face and neck. She was absolutely stunning.

"I want you," he said, *with me forever*, he didn't finish.

"Then come take me." With a wicked grin, Alice positioned her core over Christopher's length, her face tensing up and then relaxing as she took his entire length inside of her. She fit so perfectly tight around him, Christopher had to actively resist thrusting inside of her, letting her set the pace.

Slowly, Alice began moving, sliding along his length as she braced herself by leaning back onto his thighs. Christopher clasped her firm ass with both hands as she writhed on top of him. Alice rotated her hips in small circles, shooting pleasure up his body. He closed his eyes, his head falling back, a moan of delight escaping his lips.

Alice's legs shook as she continued pumping on him, and Christopher leaned forward to rub her swollen clit. She moaned at his touch, now moving faster on top of him. Christopher was enchanted, almost mesmerized at the sight of her on the brink. Alice's breath came quickly, and her entire body pulsed with anticipation.

With a scream, Alice came shuddering around him, pulsing against his hard cock with her inner walls. It took everything Christopher had not to follow her over the edge.

Alice laid her head on Christopher's chest, panting. "It may be a stupid question but..." she turned away. "Don't vampires, when they have sex..." She trailed off.

"It's okay, you can ask me anything." Christopher cradled Alice's head in his hands.

"Isn't there biting involved?" Alice turned bright red, a blush that trailed all the way down to her chest.

"Sometimes." Christopher grinned. "It's a way for us to connect, for a vampire to feel their partner's emotions with more intensity." He gently kissed Alice's neck. He could hear her pulse roaring at such a close distance and could smell her wanting. "I don't want to hurt you."

She shook her head. "I know, I trust you."

She lifted off of his cock to sit beside him on the bed. Before he could respond, her hand encircled his length, playing with the underside of the shaft and making a ring with her fingers around the tip, squeezing just enough for his back to arch and he fought with centuries of self-control to hold onto this release.

"Woman, you're going to kill me." He moaned.

"Well, I did promise you I was going to bring you to your knees."

Alice grinned at him, lying down and pulling Christopher so he crouched on his knees on top of her. She bucked her hips, raising her legs to hook over his shoulders, her core lifting to make brief contact with Christopher's length.

"I want this," she said. "All of this."

With a low growl, Christopher thrust into Alice, reveling in each sweet inch of her passage. She gasped as he moved within her, harder and faster than before. He could smell her blood as it ran excited laps around her body. Christopher's hands roamed her skin, and his canines elongated from his gums into their fully primal state. He looked Alice in the eye and she spoke a single word.

"Yes."

Christopher bit down into the flesh of Alice's shoulder, feeling her tense beneath him at the brief moment of pain. He drank deep and Alice's essence streamed into him as he continued moving inside of her. Her compassion tasted like sunlight, her enchanting view of the world, her joy, her excitement, her arousal all flowed through him. He tasted her past loneliness, her longing for a community which she couldn't quite articulate. Her dreams of endless time to learn, to explore, to see wonders washed over him. Everything about his world fascinated her, and the glimpse she'd seen into the larger supernatural community beckoned with a promise of fun, excitement, and something new.

He broke away quickly, but he had drank enough to know that he'd fallen head over heels in love with Alice. With a few stuttered thrusts he spilled his seed in her, calling out her name as she came once more in a screaming, writhing surge of humanity. He collapsed back against the pillows.

They held each other in silence for a few long heartbeats, grinning as they each caught their breath.

Christopher tasted the words on the tip of his tongue. *I love you, I want us to be together. Please stay human.*

Alice spoke first.

"This would be the perfect time for you to turn me." She snuggled into his arms a little further.

Christopher pushed down his selfish disappointment before it showed on his face. *This is her choice.* Christopher used his teeth to cut a small gash in his forearm and offered it to Alice.

"Only if you're *sure.*"

Without hesitation, Alice's lips found Christopher's arm, and she drank, the crimson liquid dripping over her lips and down her chin. Christopher felt his power passing into her, his past, his future, all irrevocably connecting him to this incredible woman. *At least now the world will have her preserved for the ages, even if I can never be with her.*

Alice looked up and delicately wiped away the blood trailing down from her mouth. "Is that enough? I'm beginning to feel a little woozy."

"Yes. It's done. You should rest now." Christopher wrapped Alice in his arms, savoring the memory of the first and last time they would ever be together.

Alice blinked awake. A note on the pillow next to her said, "Back Soon" in sweeping, old-fashioned handwriting. She smiled and stretched out on the soft silk sheets. She'd woken up a few times in the last few hours, woozy and feeling like every muscle weighed a hundred pounds, but upon waking this time she felt strong enough to lift up Christopher's four poster bed and throw it across the room.

The curtains were thrown open, revealing the sparkling brightness of the moon. Even though the room was fairly dim, everything looked brighter. Her senses were alive, the sounds of branches groaning in the wind and squirrels scratching at bark louder and more distinct than she'd ever heard before. She inhaled, and she could smell Christopher's scent imbedded in the sheets, as well as the faint burning of filament in the light bulbs of the chandelier above her. Every detail of everything around her was clearer, more beautiful than anything in her previous life.

Even her memories were sharper; the frame by frame replay of Christopher's skin, his lips, his tongue sliding and writhing with her, made her pulse race. She shifted beneath the covers, enjoying the slide of the silk against her skin. *Margot was right. Sex as a vampire will be amazing.*

She heard Christopher's footsteps approaching the top of the stairs, and she propped herself up in bed as attractively as possible. He opened the door slowly, like he was being careful of waking her, and nudged the door open with his hip while balancing a large tray between his hands.

The smell of orange juice, warm bread, and blood hit her nostrils like a wave. She'd smelled blood before once when she cut her hand cooking, the scent metallic like old pennies, but the row of red-filled shot glasses across the back of the tray Christopher carried gave off a confusing combination of scents, like she was smelling *feelings*.

Christopher smiled. "Excellent. You're awake. I brought you breakfast." He set down the tray on the end of the bed and walked over to give her a gentle kiss on the forehead.

"Thank you." She realized that she still wasn't wearing any clothes, and looked around to see a robe sitting on the bedside table beside her.

"Not a problem, it's just the beginning of getting you accustomed to all this." He settled next to the tray, keeping it between them, and averting his eyes as she pulled on the robe. Once she was relatively dressed, she crawled across the bed to join him.

"Are you regretting last night?" she asked.

His head popped up. "No! Last night was incredible, one of the best nights of my life. But it can't happen again, not now that I'm your sire."

Alice pushed down her disappointment. She'd known this was going to be the price of becoming a vampire, but that didn't make it feel any less like a rejection. The sex last night had been so much more intense than she'd anticipated, the feeling of being really *one* with him had been more than she'd ever felt with anyone else. *Had he felt the same?* She tried to distract herself by studying the tray he'd brought.

The man knew how to make a breakfast, she had to give him that. The tray was laden with a three-cheese omelet, warm cinnamon rolls dripping with icing, fresh-squeezed orange and mango juice, and a bowl of freshly-cut fruit. Across the back of the tray were six shot glasses filled with blood. The blood's intense pull sent nervous shivers of desire down her spine. *I'm a vampire. Holy shit.*

She picked up the tray. With her enhanced vampire muscles, the tray felt like it weighed almost nothing at all.

"This is way too much food," she said.

Christopher grinned. "Think of it as my welcome to your new life. Nobody should start a fresh existence on an empty stomach, especially when your body is still adjusting."

Alice took a bite of the omelet and let out a moan. Each individual ingredient and spice was amplified beyond her imagination. Every morsel tasted divine.

"Do you want some? There's enough here for at least three people," Alice said.

Christopher shook his head. "I already ate."

Alice didn't need any further encouragement. She tucked in, each bite better than the last. And yet, there was a sense of emptiness that grew the more she ate, her hunger roaring at her even as she polished off the last strawberry from the fruit salad and licked the plates clean.

"Thanks, that was amazing," she said.

"You're very welcome. There's a lot to love about this life, I hope you enjoy it." Christopher ran a hand up and down her arm. Alice relaxed into his touch.

"No broody vampires on your watch?" She smiled at him, feeling the warmth of his gaze all the way down to her toes.

Christopher laughed. "Exactly." His face lit up when he laughed. He was truly the most handsome man she'd ever seen.

"Have you ever regretted becoming a vampire?" she asked.

Christopher sat back on his elbows so he was lounging next to her on the bed with his legs hanging off the side.

"I suppose every decision comes with certain downsides. I'll never know what it feels like to grow old. The turn of the seasons doesn't have the same relief it used to; the arrival of spring loses its joy when winter seemed to pass in a moment." He touched her hand softly. "I've met so many extraordinary people only to witness them age and die in what feels like the blink of an eye. It's part of what draws me to art: it's how thoughts are preserved after the artists are gone." He sat back, his smile shaky but still there. "But I've never seen the point in focusing on the downsides of my chosen path. Life is just too long to dwell on regrets." He put his hand over hers. "Are you having doubts already?"

"No! I just woke up, and everything is amazing. You've been so kind. I'll remember fondly my first moments as a vampire forever."

Christopher looked away. "I'm very glad."

Alice put down the tray to curl up next to him. "What is it?"

"Just remembering something."

She brushed a stray lock of hair behind his ear. "Tell me." He suddenly looked so sad, so tired that she wanted to wrap him in her arms.

"I was thinking about my brother, Rhys. He and I were turned at the same time, by the same sire. Rhys wasn't a big fan of humanity. Within an hour of being turned, he slaughtered an *entire* village. Our sire didn't care. Humans were basically ants in his eyes. My first moments as a vampire were spent trying to save Rhys's victims, and I've been doing it ever since." He sat up. "But I refuse to be defined by that." He nudged the tray toward her.

He grinned again, and Alice could see the effort behind it. *Damn, I could fall in love with this man.* Her stomach sank. That wasn't an option. But everything about him called to her: his optimism and hope in the face of centuries of conflict, his kindness, and his smile. The way the moonlight hit his face transformed him into an angel, and she hungered to climb on top of him and ride his cock until she screamed.

Christopher had been talking for a couple of seconds. Alice shook herself to stop staring at his lips and actually pay attention to his words.

"--shot glasses are all blood from different types of supernaturals. You'll learn in time how to tell the difference between each kind, and how to interpret what they were feeling when they donated. For right now, let's just start with the basics."

Alice lifted one of the shot glasses and took a sniff. It smelled like soaring skies and fire, like cold scales and strength. She took a deep breath and drank down the shot in one go. A huge sense of power surged through her, and under all that, a sense of peace, joy, and contentment.

"A dragon?" Alice asked. She could barely believe that such things actually existed, and yet she loved how *full* the world was now since she gained her Sight.

Christopher clapped his hands. "Yes! That's the blood of a dragon shifter friend of mine who agreed to donate a bit for training purposes. She just got married a few weeks ago, and you should be able to smell her state of mind in addition to her species."

"We can really tell all that?" Alice asked. She tried to lean into the feelings that washed over her when she drank, but she couldn't hold onto them. She sniffed at Christopher. "Why can't I smell your emotions now that I'm a vampire?"

He tapped his nose. "That would work only if I'm human. As a vampire, my blood would have to be in the open air for you to smell it."

"I can barely believe this is really real."

"This and more." He held out another glass. "Here, try this."

Alice felt her whole body go rigid. Fear pulsed through her. She tried to say something, but her jaw was locked. Her hand lashed out, moving against her will toward the shot glass. Every cell in her body demanded that she take the glass from Christopher and consume its contents.

What is happening? She yelled the words in her head, but nothing came out. Her body wasn't her own, her hand moving against her will even as she tried with all her might to force it away from the glass. Her fingers clutched around the shot and she downed the blood in one gulp. A surge of sweetness and flowers and light and sun passed over her tongue, but Alice couldn't savor anything in her terror. As soon as she swallowed, her body returned to her in a rush, and she fell back limp against the bed.

"What was that?" Her voice sounded small and scared. "What just happened to me? I couldn't stop."

"Oh gods, Alice, I'm so sorry." Christopher's words came in an anguished rush. "I didn't mean to. It's the *hortari*. Even when I don't mean to give you a command, my words require you to do what I say." He scrambled off the bed. "This is why I stay away from the vampires I sire. You deserve your free will, to learn and grow and be your own person."

A knock at the door made them both jump.

"Christopher?" A woman's voice said from the other side of the door.

"Yes, Valerie, I'm in here." He sounded relieved.

A lovely Latina woman with black hair pulled back into a long braid that reached down to her waist opened the door. Her brow was furrowed and her tight-lipped smile looked forced. *Something's wrong.*

"Christopher, you need to get to the castle immediately." She glanced at Alice. "We'll look after the new recruit."

Christopher's face paled. He turned to lay a hand on Alice's shoulder. "I'm so sorry that things can't be different. Please feel free to explore as you wish the rest of the house and get to know the lieutenants in my sire line." He spoke slowly, like he was carefully choosing each word to make sure that nothing could be interpreted as a demand. He touched her face gently, like a farewell, and before Alice could say anything, he was gone. Valerie gave her a tight smile and followed after, leaving Alice alone.

Alice lay back against the soft sheets. Her heartbeat still raced. Both Christopher and Margot had warned her about the sire compulsion, but she hadn't realized how scary it would be to lose control of her body. It was terrifying to be *forced* to act against her will, even for something as mundane as tasting a drink she was planning on drinking anyway. Christopher's sorrow at having mistakenly used his sire power on her was sincere, but could she ever really be comfortable with him knowing that the slightest turn of phrase could strip her of her free will?

For the first time since meeting him, she understood fully why she wouldn't be able to have him in her life.

Alice shook herself. Christopher was right. There was no sense in concentrating on the negative. *Life is just too long to dwell on regrets.* She had heightened senses and super strength, and could tell how any human was feeling just by their scent.

I'm a vampire!

She certainly wasn't going to spend her first day as a vampire in bed, moping about how the one guy she wanted to be with was the one guy she couldn't have. Alice quickly got dressed in the outfit someone--probably Margot from the designer labels-- had laid out for her and headed out into the rest of the house. She followed the sound of voices through the foyer and down a hallway to a door opening up to the backyard.

She couldn't believe how *bright* the night looked. With her new vampire eyes, every detail looked as clear as if the sun shone overhead. The wide lawn looked like a set for a training montage in a Robin Hood movie. Straw dummies stuffed into vaguely humanoid shapes lined the side of the walled compound, their stuffing sticking out from knife and arrow holes all over their bodies. Padded columns serving as punching bags stood in various clumps across the space, along with various beams and gymnastics equipment for balance training.

In the middle of a marked, padded space, Margot and two men Alice didn't recognize bantered as they attacked each other in a flurry of strikes with five-foot tall staffs. They jumped and weaved around each other, the staffs almost invisible blurs, as they twirled and struck with hard cracks. Alice stared, her mouth open. She'd known Margot was a vampire, but Alice wasn't prepared to see her suave, gallery-owning friend jumping six feet in the air to aim a kick at a guy's head like an anime heroine.

Margot blocked a particularly vicious head strike and Alice squeaked in alarm. One of the men—a wiry Asian man in tight, leather pants—turned to look in the direction of the noise. It was all the distraction the other two needed to hit him simultaneously on the back and under his knees. He flew sprawling onto the pads.

"No fair!" The fallen man shouted. "Chris's newest sireling is awake."

Margot leaned on her staff, her smile wicked. "Yeah, and enemies are going to do everything they can to distract you too."

The man shrugged and jumped to his feet in a single, fluid movement. "Whatever, I'll just have to kick your ass *twice* as hard next time."

The other man, taller with dark skin and chest armor made from overlapping metal gears, laughed. "Danny, that logic makes absolutely no sense."

"It does in my head, shut up!" Danny said, smiling. He took a running leap which propelled him across the twenty-foot space between the group and Alice. He held out a hand to her. "I'm Danny. Adventurer and lover and forever at your service."

"Lay off. She's barely hours old," Margot said. She walked over to join them, with the gear-plated man close behind. "You'll make her regret joining our motley crew."

"Please ignore them." The taller man said. His voice was deep, with a measured, calm quality that radiated a sense of peace around him. He nodded to Alice, but kept his distance. "I'm Ben." He shrugged. "I'm the mad scientist of the group."

Alice stared. Except for the overlapping gears crisscrossing his chest, she would have believed he was a monk before she would ever label him as mad.

Margot punched his shoulder. "Don't call yourself that!" She winked at him. "You're the mad *genius* of the group, get it right."

"Hey, I thought I was the mad genius?" Danny said.

Margot shook her head. "No, you're just insane."

"Oh yeah, that makes more sense." Danny laughed. "Come on, let's see what you've got." In one motion, he drew a knife from a thigh holster and threw it directly at Alice's chest.

Time slowed.

Alice watched the knife coming at her, moon glinting off the metal, the movement so slow it was an easy dance to step away from the point's path and grab the knife from the air.

The group applauded. "She's a natural!" Margot cried.

Alice looked down at the knife in her hand, still amazed at what had just happened. She'd *snatched a knife from midair*. She looked back at Danny.

"You...that could have..."

Danny grinned. "You're immortal. Even if you *were* too slow, a knife wound to the chest wouldn't kill you; it would only hurt like hell. Although, for the record, you should stay away from beheading or fire; those will keep you down permanently." He walked over to a table covered with swords, axes, knives of several sizes, and a machete. He grabbed the axe and hurled it like a Frisbee at one of the straw dummies against the wall. It chopped the head straight off, the stuffing landing with a soft thump on the ground.

Alice's stomach plummeted. It might have just been a dummy's head this time, but what had she signed up for? Did they really expect her to kill someone? She was a photographer!

"I'm not so sure about all this," Alice said. The table of weapons was intimidating in itself. She pointed at a pile of acorn-sized cylinders that, with her enhanced vampire senses, smelled like harsh chemicals and something else, elusive and tantalizing. "I don't even know what half of these things are."

Ben picked up one of the cylinders. "These are my UV flash bombs. Sunlight can weaken us, so I've duplicated the effects of the sun's rays on whatever vampire they hit. These are non-fatal rounds; they just hurt like crazy. With enough exposure, they can knock an enemy unconscious long enough to make a hasty retreat." He tossed it in the air and Alice fought the instinct to jump away from it. "I'm very proud of these babies." He handed one to her. "Check it out!"

Alice recoiled away from it. "I don't know..."

Margot walked up to give Alice a gentle pat on the shoulder. "I know it's a lot all at once." She gave Ben a hard stare. "Let's start off easy before we move up to the pyrotechnics, shall we?" Margot picked up a sword from the table and handed it to Alice. "Try this. You've got a swordmaiden look about you."

"Who do you expect me to fight?" Alice's hands were shaking.

"Right now? Nobody. But living a life that lasts centuries pretty much guarantees you'll come across one danger or another. The only expectation we have is for you to be able to defend yourself."

Alice had to admit, the sword felt good in her hand. The handle was a simple grip with a metal hemisphere protecting her hand and wrist like she'd seen in old Three Musketeer movies. Although it was a solid, three-foot metal blade, she held the weight easily. She whipped the sword around the air a few times, enjoying the swishing sound as it cut the air.

"Hold on there, little vamp, you're not chopping wood," Danny said. He came up to stand next to her, rearranging her grip so that her thumb guided the blade like it was an extension of her arm.

Margot picked up another of the blades, standing opposite Alice. "All right, I'm going to show you a couple of attacks."

Margot was patient with Alice's many questions as she explained footwork, how to parry, and how to attack, with Danny and Ben giving a running commentary of their various run-ins with past foes. Danny especially seemed to run into confrontations at least once a week, a fact which Ben gently scolded him about.

They both cheered when Alice managed to clumsily recreate a feint, and she swelled with pride. Alice looked between Margot, Danny, and Ben. The connection of their family was so strong, it was like an invisible force joining them together.

This is the best part of being a vampire, she realized. *I'm a part of this.*

"Oh good, you found them."

Alice turned toward the voice, and the Latina woman, Valerie, who had called Christopher away joined them in the courtyard. Something in Valerie's expression made Margot's shoulders immediately tense. Margot always played it so cool, Alice found it unnerving to see the gallery owner looking unsure.

Valerie smiled warily at Alice. "Christopher wanted to make sure you made it out okay."

"He thought she couldn't make it down a flight of stairs?" Danny asked.

Valerie's smile widened. "I think our sire just wanted to make sure our newest member was *satisfied* with her transition." She leaned hard enough on the word to make everybody chuckle and Alice blush.

"It's not like that--" Alice started to say.

"Not anymore it's not," Margot said. "Christopher's just too good a guy to bang somebody he has absolute control over. We all know that would be a recipe for disaster." Her tone indicated the topic was closed, and it was Ben who changed the subject, turning to Valerie.

"What's the news from the palace? What has Christopher out of here so early?"

Valerie's grin died. "It's the king. He's dead."

They all started talking at once, their questions overlapping on top of one another.

"What?"

"How?"

"When?"

"You couldn't have led with that?" Danny cried.

"What are we going to do?" Margot said last.

Alice looked between them, her heart beginning to beat faster in alarm. *The king?*

Valerie held up her hands for silence. "We just got word an hour ago. It was a freak accident at the palace. We told him time and time again not to decorate his walls with ceremonial blades, but the king never bothered to listen to the opinions of others." Valerie rolled her eyes. "Christopher is headed there now to investigate and confirm the plan for succession."

"He's going *right now* with no backup?" Margot sounded outraged. She buckled the sword to her waist and grabbed a couple of UV bombs from the table. She pointed at Danny. "Come on!"

Danny nodded, and the two raced away.

Alice watched them disappear with a growing sense of alarm.

"What's going on?" She asked the rest.

Valerie looked at her sadly. "I'm sorry this is happening today of all days. As the king's last remaining sirelings, Christopher and Rhys are the heirs. It's really a matter of who claims the throne and who can hold it. Christopher is the oldest so he'll get priority, but..." Valerie paused. "If Rhys becomes king, we're all *very* fucked."

"The king's death means there's going to be a war," Ben said.

Valerie jumped in. "There *might* be a war."

"War?" The sword suddenly felt heavy in Alice's hand. She looked down at the decapitated dummy head. "Now?"

Valerie shook her head. "No, there will be a lot of negotiations and diplomacy first, but the king..." Her voice trailed off. Ben laid a hand on her shoulder. "He was an ornery old bastard who held onto outdated traditions. But he's been the king for as long as I've been alive. It's hard to believe he's really gone."

Ben twirled a small dagger in his hand, over and over like he couldn't stop. "It will be all right, you'll see. Margot and Danny were the first vampires Christopher turned, they're the strongest of us all. With them as backup, Christopher should be fine."

"But can't we help in some way?" Alice asked.

Valerie bit her lip. "Any more than those two would look like an attack, and might put all of them in danger." She sounded like she was mostly trying to convince herself. "We can help by staying here and rallying the troops. Let's call our sirelings, and they'll call *their* sirelings and we'll all get ready, in case the worse should happen."

Alice looked between them. "What's the worst that could happen?"

Valerie and Ben shared a loaded look. "Rhys being Rhys."

Mourners stood dozens thick outside the looming iron gates of the ancient royal castle as Christopher's car approached. Black flags bearing the family crest hung from the castle's Gothic turrets at half-mast, and the grounds felt strangely quiet, like even the birds who lived in the gardens knew death hung in the air.

Christopher had passed through these same gates regularly for centuries, and it never felt like this. He instinctively began to rehearse what to say to the king to try and knock him from the dark ages, but then Christopher remembered that there would be no arguments this time. His sire was dead.

Christopher rubbed a hand across his forehead. There hadn't been a new vampire king in over two millennia, but his sire's advisors would probably insist on following the rarely-used ancient rituals for mourning a monarch: months of dark clothing and plodding ceremonies as the advisors handled any business pending from the former king's rule. After that, the eldest prince would be educated at great length on trade deals, treaties, and taxes. The pomp would be endless, and Christopher already dreaded every minute of it.

The only upside he saw in the coming months was that he could finally start building a new, progressive future for his people. He drummed his fingers against the car's window. With a slow transition, Christopher hoped he could convince the remaining traditionally-minded folks to start thinking more inclusively, and he could give his people the prosperous future they deserved.

Twin motorcycles gunned down the drive at breakneck speed as Christopher got out of the car, and he tensed until he recognized Danny and Margot's helmets. They jumped off their motorcycles, grabbing weapons out of duffle bags and arming themselves to the teeth with swords and machetes lashed to their sides for easy reach.

"What are you doing here?" Christopher asked as Margot strapped a second knife to her forearm. "This visit is just a formality to see my sire's body and start planning for the transition." He looked at the bulges along her belt. "Are those grenades?"

Margot raised an eyebrow at him. "Didn't you hear? Grenades are the new black--"

"Except with a lot more fire," Danny finished, securing a machete to his thigh.

"This really isn't necessary--" Christopher started to say.

"Just think of us as your backup plan. You will be damned happy to see these grenades if your brother tries some shit," Margot said.

Christopher threw up his hands as he started up the stairs towards the castle. Margot and Danny walked on each side of him. The rhythmic tattoo of metal hitting metal as their weapons struck against armor sounded more comforting than Christopher wanted to admit. The castle, usually bustling with activity, was too quiet. *Where are the funeral planners and staff to set up the castle for mourners?*

Christopher's unease only grew as they approached the throne room. Strikingly large guards he didn't recognize stood along both sides of the hallway, easily three times as many than were necessary. Four of them blocked the double-doors to the throne room. Margot and Danny tensed on either side of him and Christopher's hand itched to grab for weapons he hadn't thought he'd need.

"Who are you?" The guard who stepped forward from the door had muscles the size of basketballs, no neck, and lips so thin his sharp canines dipped down outside his mouth like a stray dog.

Danny slid forward before Christopher got the chance to speak, stepping in between him and the guard. "This is Prince Christopher, you disrespectful, no-neck--"

"There's no need for that." Christopher moved forward. He eyed the guard. The vampire had the unsteady look of the newly turned. With all that muscle mass, he'd be a challenge to take down, but Christopher had no doubt that he, Margot, and Danny would be more than a match for the goons blocking the door. The other thirty vamps behind them would be a bigger problem.

He placed a calming hand on Danny's shoulder. "I am here to speak with my brother and pay my respects to my sire. Let us pass."

The guard shared a smirk with the others at the door and the one nearest the handle pulled the mighty-oak door open with a loud groan.

"Yeah, sure, your highness," the guard chuckled. "The king has been looking forward to this."

Christopher's unease transformed into dread. *The king?*

The throne room was the same as Christopher remembered it: gray, echoing, and cold with arched ceilings and stone gargoyles snarling from every corner. Dust hung in the air, and Christopher heard the sound of weeping from down another hallway.

Christopher's longing for a weapon grew with each second. His sire's advisors knelt on the floor along one side of the wall, their hands chained together. Guards stood over the advisors, brandishing axes and frigid expressions. There was no sign of Christopher's sire's coffin, and the royal throne was already occupied.

Rhys sneered down at his brother, one leg slung over the side of the throne's golden arm, his boots swinging with glee. Rhys's short, blonde hair lay slicked back on his head, the grease reflecting off the candlelight beside him. Christopher ground his teeth, fighting for a civil tone.

"What are you doing on our sire's throne?" Christopher eyed his brother's heavily-armed cadre of guards as he spoke. He could see Margot and Danny move closer out of the corner of his eye to guard his back, weapons at the ready.

Rhys wriggled where he sat. "It's quite a comfortable perch. I can see why he liked it so much." His jocular tone had an edge like a sabre.

He's insane. Dread and fear coiled in Christopher's chest. He looked toward the chained advisors. They had been his sire's friends for centuries, men and women who had helped *raise* them both. *What could Rhys possibly be thinking?*

"Let them go." His fists clenched in an effort to appear calm. "Even if you will not listen to their counsel, you cannot leave them like this for the funeral."

"There isn't going to be a funeral." Rhys's foot swung back and forth, his voice smooth like he was commenting on the weather. "Our dear sire's body was already burned this morning, his ashes scattered in the garden. We're done with him."

Shock hit Christopher like a petrification spell. Margot and Danny made small noises of concern behind him, but the world seemed unstable around him and he couldn't move to comfort them. Christopher's mouth gaped open and he fought to find words.

"What? But...you can't...you..."

"I think you'll find I can. My coronation is in three days, and I don't need that old bag of bones just lying around."

"I am the rightful heir to that throne," Christopher said. "Our sire is dead. In response to news of such a tragedy, you do not mourn him, you do not comfort your sire line. You instead seek to usurp my position with this..." Christopher gestured at Rhys's guards, "attempt at intimidation."

Rhys blew a bubble with his gum, a bright pink orb that expanded out six inches before snapping. He picked the bits off his nose with a manic grin.

"Who do I need to intimidate? You? Those freaks you've turned? You've spent your centuries turning poets and outcasts." He gestured at a large man with tattoos of barbed wire circling his bald head and neck. "This big bastard here was a champion powerlifter before I made him part of my sire line. Now his will is mine. What chance do your ballerinas have against a force like him?"

Rhys hopped off the throne and strode toward him. Margot and Danny moved to block him, but Christopher extended his hand to stop them from interfering. Rhys's eyes were crazy, his long fingers taking Christopher's chin in a tight grip.

"All of your little, artsy farsty, riff raff sirelings," Rhys said in a sing-song tone, "are *ruining* what it means to be a vampire." He shouted the last words, spit flecking out in all directions.

Christopher pried Rhys's hand from his face. "My sirelings are none of your business."

Rhys tsked as he jumped back to delicately perch on the throne once more. "They're my business when you refuse to hold them to your will. You let your pets run around with no leash." He spat on the stone floor. "It's an *embarrassment*. How could a sire like you rule our people? You can't even rule your own line." He pointed to the guards poised next to the kneeling advisors. They weren't quite as beefcake as Rhys's new personal guards, but they all had the same vacant expressions. "Do you see my new sirelings? I selected these lucky bastards into my command because those old farts at their feet are their drinking buddies and mentors." He raised his hand and brought down like a falling guillotine. "Kill them."

Before Christopher could move, the guards' swords chopped off the heads of the kneeling advisors. The decapitated bodies of his sire's most trusted confidants fell to the stone floor with sickening, wet thumps. Rhys's hold broken the moment they fulfilled the command, the guards holding the swords immediately started to shake and sputter in shock. One started to vomit, another fell to the ground, sobbing.

"Fucking hell," Danny cursed behind Christopher, his voice small with shock and horror.

"I can take them," Margot said, quiet enough that only Christopher could hear.

"I'm so sorry! I'm so sorry! I'm so sorry!" One guard wailed over and over.

"Shut up!" Rhys yelled and his guards all froze silently in place, tears and horror cemented on their faces. Rhys leaned back onto his throne and crossed his legs. "Anyone who disagrees with me is going to face the same consequences."

Rage and shame circled in a whirlwind inside Christopher.

"This isn't over." If they stayed in the room any longer, Christopher knew he wouldn't be able to stop Margot, Danny, or himself from attacking Rhys, and they were hopelessly outnumbered. They needed a plan. Christopher pulled Margot and Danny out of the throne room, their footsteps echoing against the empty stone walls.

They didn't speak until they'd gotten outside and the moonlit sky was a welcome relief from the castle's weight.

"Well...that's not great." Margot's voice broke the silence.

Danny ran a hand through his short, black hair. "I don't know why we didn't just kill him right there."

"We will stop him." Christopher stood tall now, steady in his conviction. "But first, we need to get out of here. Now."

Christopher barely remembered the car ride back. Danny and Margot drove their motorcycles in front and behind of his car to keep watch in case Rhys sent one of his mind-wiped minions to run Christopher off the road. Rhys had always been reckless with his use of the *hortari*, but Christopher had never believed his brother would go this far. The sound of the heads hitting the floor, immediately followed by the anguished cries of their friends who couldn't resist Rhys's command, was a miserable loop repeating in his memory.

Rhys has to be stopped.

As soon as they arrived home, Christopher asked an anxious-looking Danny and Margot to gather the lieutenants in the dining room. Shouts of horror reverberated throughout the house as his sirelings learned of Rhys's actions. Christopher ransacked his rooms, dumped boxes out of storage and gathered as many floor plans and charts of the castle that he could find. He was about to ask his sirelings, his family, to engage in a full-scale assault against a fortified castle, and he couldn't leave anything to chance.

Christopher was in the midst of unrolling each map along the long, wooden dining table, and weighing down the edges with coasters and candlesticks when his sirelings filed in. Margot came first, taking her place at his right hand, and nodding to Danny, Ben, and Valerie as they ringed the rest of the table, their expressions grave. The dining room wasn't outfitted as a war room--the pastoral paintings of hillsides weren't exactly the scenes to inspire battle-- but it was the only room with a big enough table for all the maps scattered across its surface.

I'm not outfitted for war, Christopher thought with a nervous twinge.

A moment later, Alice slipped in behind them. Christopher's heart skipped a beat in terror. He left the table to pull her aside.

"I don't want you anywhere near this," he said. "Whatever we decide here today, you shouldn't be a part of it." He tried to push down images of Alice mangled on the battlefield. Alice being torn to shreds by Rhys's men. Alice broken and dying all because Christopher wanted to be king.

She raised her chin and pulled her arm out of his grip. "If you didn't want me to be a part of this, then you shouldn't have made me one of you. I have a right to be here."

Christopher looked at his other sirelings. Margot, Danny, Ben, and Valerie had spent decades learning to fight. At one time or another, they'd had to defend themselves or someone else, but they'd never seen real war. Thinking of any of them hurt was like a stabbing pain through his heart. But if Rhys became king, his choices would harm them too. They deserved the right to choose their fate. He touched Alice's hand, needing the comforting contact of her touch.

"You're right," he said in a quiet voice.

He took a deep breath and stepped back to the front of the table. Christopher's sirelings were already pouring over the blueprints and maps spread across the table. He tried to keep his eyes off of Alice as she took an open space between Margot and Ben, looking down at the plans.

"Thank you all for joining me." He straightened his spine and raised his voice to be easily heard throughout the room. "I'm sure by now that you've all heard that my sire, your king, has died."

Somber murmurs made small laps around the room. Margot banged her fist down on the table for silence.

"As his eldest sireling, I am the rightful heir to that throne. As vampires, we can never age, but that does not mean we cannot grow." Christopher calmly clasped his hands in front of him. "We must ensure our values of freedom, independent expression, and respect for all are protected. The vampire community must know that, although the *hortari* is a reality of our existence, it does not give anyone the right to enslave others." Christopher smiled a thin smile, dreading what he must ask of them all. "Rhys has seized the throne as his own, muscling his way to sovereignty. He threatens to make legions of *hortari*-locked slaves to carry out his whims. We must prove that our way is stronger."

"And how do we do that?" Valerie asked.

"We are going to take back the castle."

"Okaaayyy," Danny said slowly. "How?"

Christopher smiled. "That's the point. The ability of each of us to think for ourselves is what will preserve our ideals." He outstretched his hands to encompass the table of maps and drawings of the castle. "We're going to combine our skills to build a plan *together*. Rhys's coronation is in three days. I need you to bring in everyone you need, and consult with every contact you have. We are stronger because we are together, and we *will* win."

The whole table broke out into cheers and applause. Christopher's heart swelled with pride at their loyalty, but his gaze was irrevocably drawn back to Alice, her head bowed in intense conversation with Ben at the far end of the room.

He walked along the length of the table watching the others jump into action. Margot and Valerie pulled maps toward themselves and started to point out weaknesses in the outer structure, while Danny scanned the lists of castle employees and made notes on his tablet. Christopher cared for all of them, but Alice looked so vulnerable next to his years-hardened sirelings, his chest ached with worry.

"Alice, what do you think about checking out my dark room?" Christopher told Alice once he'd reached her side. "You can start to develop some new photos. We're safe here for now, you don't have to stick around for all the planning." He pressed his hand to the small of her back, guiding her towards the exit.

"Are you going to use your UV flash bombs?" Alice slid out of Christopher's grasp, returning to the table next to Ben, taking a device about the size of a roll of quarters out of the inventor's hand. She seemed to be studiously ignoring Christopher, her gaze fixed on the delicate glass and steel structure.

Christopher couldn't smell her emotions now that she was a vampire the way he'd been able to when she was a human, but he recognized the tightness in her jaw and the hunch in her shoulders as signs of fear.

She shouldn't be doing this. Alice was an artist. She didn't have the training for war. Of all his sirelings, she was the most likely to get hurt, and the thought terrified him more than he thought was possible.

Ben smiled at Alice. "You don't have to be so gentle with it, this one's inactive." Ben pointed down at the blueprints of the royal throne room. "If we set them up to blast here, here, and here." He pointed to three different sections of the page. "We should be able to knock 'em back a bit."

"Hmmm." Alice bit on her thumb, then pulled some loose change out of her pocket and placed the coins down onto the map. "You've got a really good strategy, *but* there's an opportunity to miss some of Rhys's men in the shadows you've created here and here. If you install the UV flash bombs where I've put these coins, they will overlap so every inch of the throne room will be covered."

Ben tilted his head to examine the new placement of the coins. "That's brilliant!" Ben clapped Alice on the shoulder proudly. "How did you know to do that?"

Alice smiled. "When I first started taking pictures, learning proper lighting was rough. But now I'm a bit of an expert."

"A lighting expert! Good thinking, bringing this one in, Christopher." Ben laughed heartily. "They'll never see it comin'."

Margot leaned over, "What's this? Our photo prodigy is going to help us UV the crap out of these douchebags?"

"Just in the initial planning," Christopher growled. "She's not trained for battle."

Ben shrugged and Alice opened her mouth like she was about to say something, but Margot tapped her arm and shook her head. Alice glanced at Christopher and blushed, then went back to studying the blueprints, moving the coins slightly on the map and edging around the table to look at the picture from a different angle. The light from the chandelier elongated the shadows under her eyes like she was already dead.

No, not her. Never her. Christopher circled the room to put some distance between himself and

Alice, knowing he was being selfish trying to minimize her involvement. He couldn't stop thinking that making her a vampire had been supposed to preserve Alice and keep her from harm. Now she was helping them plan for battle.

Danny looked up from a debate with Valerie about whether it was worth trying to proactively turn some of Rhys's sirelings to their cause before the battle when he saw Christopher approach. Danny lightheartedly elbowed Christopher in the ribs.

"Hey there, Chris. It's nice having us all together, admit it."

"Even if I'm marching you to your probable deaths?" Christopher asked.

"Even if."

"I do enjoy seeing you all, being together as a family but..." Christopher sighed, "Just the other day I accidentally rendered Margot mute, just from a careless word. This damn *hortari* makes me a danger to all of you."

"I'm not sure if shutting up Margot for a moment is *such* a bad thing." Danny ducked out of the way of a flying candlestick thrown with impressive speed. "Just kidding." He waved his hands in surrender. "It doesn't *have* to be this way. I've heard stories of vamps breaking the *hortari*."

"That's what they are, stories." Christopher ran his hand through his short, dark hair and gripped at the ends in frustration. "The *hortari* bond is unbreakable, and Rhys is going to use it to enslave everyone around him." Christopher looked around the room. How many would still be alive when all of this was over? "We will have to call on everybody we can trust, every ally."

"My sirelings have sirelings," Danny said. "Gotta love that exponential growth."

Christopher plunged a knife into the nearest blueprint. "We're going to need every advantage we can get."

Alice stared at the knife wedged deep into the table. It cut through the throne. *Not a comforting image.* Christopher and his sirelings were still discussing battle strategies and how to ensure safe avenues of retreat. For all that Christopher turned people he respected as artisans, they were also all trained warriors and had lived long enough to learn a few things about strategy.

I want to join the battle.

She wasn't sure when she'd come to the realization. Sure, Alice had always wanted to help, but actually being part of a physical assault? It was almost unthinkable. It might have been seeing Christopher pace around the room with fear etched in the lines around his eyes. Or hearing him stand amidst his people and *request* support in a room full of vampires who would have no choice but to help if he had been less careful in his wording. Christopher was a good man, and the sirelings he'd created were some of the most fun and clever people she'd ever known. The thought of any of them getting hurt made her feel sick.

Alice slid her coins on the map of the throne room, adjusting it slightly. She bit her lip. There were so many variables that would come into play when positioning the flash bombs. The blueprints showed how tall the room was and where the windows were positioned, but there could be any number of factors that might impact the reach of the UV rays.

"I have to go with you," Alice said.

Danny and Margot were in a loud argument about the comparative merit of spears in the coronation room versus their uselessness in the tight castle corridors.

Alice raised her voice to be heard. "I'm going to come with you to the coronation."

"That's ridiculous," Christopher said.

Danny and Margot stopped arguing. Margot turned to Alice and pursed her lips.

"You're barely turned, Alice," Margot said. "That makes you weaker than every vampire there. You might be good with that sword with a few more years of training, but you're nowhere near ready, hon."

"I didn't turn you so you could die a week later." Christopher's voice sounded final.

"You don't get it," Alice said. "Those UV bombs. You're going to need me there to maximize their reach."

"Ben can handle it. He invented them," Christopher said.

Ben raised his hand. "Actually, Ben can't." Christopher scowled at him. "Look, I just make the contraptions. I leave it up to you guys to use them to the best of your abilities. My expertise is in chemical reactions and mechanics, not light distribution."

"It's not happening," Christopher said. He looked around the room. "And that's final."

"But--" Alice started to say.

Christopher held up a hand. "Stop."

Alice's entire body locked in place, her mouth clicking shut as Christopher's sire compulsion took control.

She struggled to move, sweat beading on her forehead at the effort. She concentrated on the specific command. *He said 'stop', not 'stop talking'.*

"My liege, can I talk to you a second?" The words took effort to leave her mouth, but since his command had been so unspecific, Alice managed to form the words.

Christopher pulled his fingers through his hair. He let out a long breath. "Yes, sorry. We can talk outside." He looked at the others. "All of you, you know what to do. We'll meet again tomorrow to compare numbers and continue to fine-tune the plan."

The sirelings all shared significant looks and filed out. Christopher held open the door for Alice and walked beside her until they were outside on the front porch. Her car from the day before--which felt like a million years ago--was still parked at the end of the driveway.

Alice waited until she heard the last of the other sirelings leave and they were alone before turning back to Christopher.

"You need me there. Not bringing me puts the others at risk."

Christopher shook his head. "Are you so determined to die?" His voice grew louder with each word.

Alice stepped toward him, determined to calm him down. "You gave me immortality so that I could have more chances to do *good* in this world. Helping stop your brother is exactly that."

"Rhys is my problem, not yours. Your death is Not. An. Option." Christopher stepped so close, his breath brushed against her face. Everything in her body felt charged being near him. Her muscles practically vibrated with a need to touch him: to comfort or slap him, she wasn't sure.

She pressed her palm against his cheek. "This is my choice. I'm going with you."

He pulled her closer, his mouth pressing against hers in sudden desperation. His tongue pushed into her mouth, and she opened to him, grabbing his shoulders to pull herself close. His fingers laced through her hair, tangling in the strands, while his other hand cupped her ass. She shivered with pleasure.

He felt so *right*, so perfect against her body. All day she'd been trying to not think about their night together, but it all rushed back at the feel of his hands, the scent of him surrounding her, her enhanced vampire senses making every detail of him more intense.

He broke away from the kiss, still holding her close. "Don't you understand? I can't lose you. You mean so much to me, more than anyone ever has. I need you to be safe." She started to protest, but he looked deep into her eyes. "Get in your car, Alice. Drive away and live your life the way you choose, but never look for me. I will never come near you again. This is my last command to you. Go." He stepped away from her.

"No!" But it was too late, the *hortari* had already taken control. Every muscle in her body forced her towards her car. "Christopher, stop this!" She pushed back against the compulsion with everything she could, her mind screaming as she tried to gain control of a body that kept putting one foot in front of another in an irrevocable march.

Christopher stood behind her, tears in his eyes and grief etched in every line of his face, but he didn't come any closer.

Nightmare images flashed through her mind. The bright light of the UV bombs missing key areas of the room, Rhys's faceless evil minions descending on Christopher and his sire line, their fangs dripping with blood like some B horror movie. All because she wasn't there. Danny dead. Valerie dead. Ben dead. Margot dead.

Christopher dead.

"No! I need to stay!" She looped her arms around one of the lamp posts that lined the side of the driveway and held on with all her might. With every second she tried to resist the *hortari*'s pull, the pain increased. Her shoulders ached as her lower body pulled towards the car. A hot heaviness was forcing itself up from her feet through her legs and into her stomach, magma filling her limbs. She locked her arms around the pole as her legs throbbed in pain as they tried to walk away. She lowered herself to the ground, one hand under the other, until she lay flat on her stomach and her feet could only kick spasmodically behind her.

"What are you doing?" Christopher asked. He came closer, his expression a mix of curiosity and awe.

She closed her eyes, shutting out the pain, letting a growing fury push back against the weight of hot magma burning up her chest and into her neck. Alice screamed, the sound breaking through the agony.

"This is such *bullshit*!" Fury like she'd never felt pulsed through her. This was her body. This was her *will*. She had to *break* this.

Memories swirled. Christopher kissing her. Christopher carrying her to his bed. The pleasure shooting through her as she came over and over against at the feel of his mouth. Christopher's face when he told her they could never be together because it was his blood that made her a vampire. Everything about her new existence was perfect, could be perfect, if she could only break through this.

The pain was agonizing, but she leaned into it now. Somewhere inside herself, Alice looked straight at the pain, acknowledged it, welcomed it. This was a goddamn staring contest from hell and there was no way she was about to blink.

I can do this.

One in a million broke the sire bond, but there was always that one.

The pain tried to take over, pain spiking into her. She screamed again, a mindless wail of agony that was nowhere near accepting defeat.

I can do this.

Blackness tinged her vision, and Alice felt like she was passing out. *No, that's the hortari.* She fought against it, looking up into Christopher's face. He was smiling now, laughing almost, tears rolling down his face.

"I can't believe it," he said. "You're amazing."

She held on, pushing against the blackness, focusing on his smile.

The *hortari* shattered.

She collapsed limp against the ground.

The pain disappeared, leaving only a dull ache in her limbs from all the strain and the kicking. The pull to leave was gone.

She shakily got to her feet, dusting off the gravel that stuck to her arms and side.

"Tell me to do something," she said, her voice breathless with hope and anticipation.

Christopher shook off his shock. "Um, I don't know. Touch your nose."

She waited a second to see if she felt anything, but there was nothing. Alice wiggled her fingers freely in front of Christopher's face.

"Nope! Not gonna do it!" She laughed and jumped forward into his arms, kissing him furiously. He kissed her back, pulling her closer and carrying her to the house, her legs straddling his waist and her arms wrapped around his shoulders.

"No one..." He said in between kisses to her mouth, her neck, her cheek. "No one has ever fought so hard for me. I didn't think it was possible."

She roughly pulled a fistful of his hair, forcing his head back, while pressing her chest closer so her hard nipples rubbed against the front of his jacket.

"It wasn't all for you. I was fighting for my freedom." She pressed her lips against his, moaning when his mouth opened for her and her tongue battled against his for dominance. "And for this." She reached down to stroke his erect cock pressing against her stomach.

He looked around. They were still in the middle of the driveway. The others would be returning at any time with their reinforcements.

"Race you to the bedroom," she said, dropping to her feet and running with her enhanced vampire speed back into the house.

"No fair! You got a head start!"

She was already so far in front of him, she could barely hear his words. Alice raced up the stairs and down the hallway at a speed that reduced the house's carefully-curated decorations into a tasteful blur. She kicked open the bedroom door and spun in time to grab hold of Christopher and use his momentum to toss him onto the bed. He sprawled against the headboard and she jumped onto him, tearing off her shirt and bra in a single rip and pressing her nipple against his mouth. He sucked and licked at her command, the shuddering pleasure running through her not stopping as he managed to pull apart his shirt without breaking contact. He switched his attention from one breast to another, licking and sucking her nipples to tight points.

She could feel every indent on his tongue, every hair on his arms where they wrapped around her back. His aroused scent made wetness pool between her legs, demanding she become closer to him. Enhanced strength made ripping off his pants, the fabric tearing like paper, all the easier. Her own pants came next until they were both bare.

"Alice, you're---"

"Shut up." She pressed him down against the bed, positioning her pussy above his mouth. "I'm still pissed at you for *commanding* me to leave."

"I'm at your command now. Whatever you want, I'm yours. Forever." He grabbed her hips, pulling her wet mound towards him so he could lick her clit, his tongue making wide sweeps along her slit, exploring all her folds. Spikes of pleasure rushed through her every time his tongue flicked her bud.

"Yes, that," she panted.

He flicked her clit again, and Alice couldn't help but thrust until she was riding his face in wild gyrations, her clit rubbing against his nose, his mouth, his lips. The intensity of the sensations was more than she'd ever felt before; every place they touched thrilled her, drove her on.

"Oh gods, I'm coming!" she screamed, just as he thrust his tongue deep into her, fucking her deep, as his fingers danced against her clit. She came in waves, lights flashing behind her eyes as she spasmed on top of his face. When the waves slowed, she sat back. His face glistened with her cum and he licked his lips. She leaned forward and tasted herself on his mouth. Behind her, his enormous cock strained upwards, brushing against her ass.

It felt too gorgeous to resist. She turned to lean down and lick along his shaft, wrapping her lips around his tip. Christopher gripped the sheets so tight, the fabric threatened to tear.

"Careful, I'm so close," he said.

She grabbed his cock with her hand, using his pre-cum to lubricate her palm as she stroked him up and down with fast, measured strokes. His cock jumped and she licked along the tip, putting gentle pressure on the underside and licking upward. His chest vibrated with tension between her thighs. She lifted her head, letting go of his shaft just before he came. She jumped off to kneel beside him. He looked so gorgeous laying there. He was the most exquisite being she'd ever seen. *And he's mine.*

He reached for her. "Tell me, what do you need?" he asked.

She crawled closer, straddling his cock. She locked eyes with him as she lowered herself down onto his shaft. He was so big, his cock stretched at her walls.

"You. I need all of you."

He moaned, his hands massaging her breasts as he thrust up into her wet heat.

She leaned down and bit his lip, rolling her hips so his stomach brushed against her clit with each movement. His cock felt amazing buried deep inside her, every part of them connected. She remembered her last night as a human, the perfection of him inside her. And this time, it wasn't their final chance, it was just the beginning.

She came screaming Christopher's name, bliss infusing every limb as she let the pleasure wash over her. Christopher's thrusts under her became more urgent until he was groaning loudly and she felt him spill inside of her.

"Yesssss." She curled up on top of him, feeling him slowly go soft while still inside her. She touched his face. "This is worth everything."

He kissed her gently. "I wish I could keep you safe."

Alice smiled, kissing his nose. "I appreciate that, but if protecting me means taking away my choices, then we're going to have problems."

He grinned. "Well, even if the *hortari* isn't working, I could still tie you up to keep you from joining the battle."

"Haha, by that logic, I should tie *you* up so you don't get hurt either." She wiggled her hips a little.

"*That* image I don't mind at all." His hands started to roam her back. "Taking turns with the cuffs..." His hands found her wrists, pulled them together and back behind her so her chest arched back and he could lean up to kiss her breasts.

She laughed. "Keep that up, and neither of us will ever leave."

He licked her nipple. "Perhaps that's the best option." Christopher's smile dimmed and he leaned back against the pillows, releasing her wrists. "Unfortunately, Rhys is a problem that I have to fix."

"Why does it have to be you?" She dismounted his cock and curled up next to him, spooning against him. She pulled up the sheet so its smooth fabric cocooned them both.

"Rhys and I are more than just sired by the same vampire, we were born brothers. He's always been selfish and power-mad, and I've always tried to protect others from him. We weren't born rich, our family herded sheep, and Rhys always seemed to resent it. One of the few memories I still have from when I was human is from when I was sixteen or seventeen and Rhys was fifteen or so. There was this girl in our town born with a cleft lip that partially deformed her face. Really nice girl, amazing weaver." Christopher took a deep breath. "Rhys convinced the other boys in the village that she was evil, that they could prove their strength as men if they hurt her. I did everything I could to protect her, but once the idea circulated far enough through town, there was no stopping the attacks. I managed to safely smuggle her out of town and place her with some distant aunts. But it always haunted me, how Rhys's cruelty managed to alter somebody's life so drastically. It was the first time I saw something like that, but definitely not the last." Christopher leaned back against the bed's headrest, closing his eyes. "With our sire's death, Rhys and I are the oldest vampires still alive. I can't let him have influence over the direction of our people and I'm the only one with a strength that equals his own." His breath stirred Alice's hair and she cuddled closer to him. She ached at the pain in his voice.

"Then you need all the help you can get to stop him." She pulled at his hand so it reached around her and rested on her stomach.

He gripped her hand. "I do. I was scared and selfish and tried to keep you safe at the expense of the success of the battle. You're right, though. You have a talent that will be invaluable in battle. Without you, my sirelings could end up hurt or worse." Christopher's fingers caressed her stomach. "I just... I'm terrified at the thought of you getting harmed."

"Why is that?"

He sat up on one arm so he could look down at her face. "You want me to say it, don't you?"

"We're going into battle," she reminded him, turning so their eyes were level. "If there's anything you want off your chest, you should say it now."

He kissed her, his lips attacking hers as he pulled her closer. He pulled her leg up over him so they were wrapped together on their sides in the bed. His cock was hard against her opening, and all it took was just a slightly different angle of his hips and he slid inside her from behind in one smooth stroke. He started to thrust gently into her, holding her so close his cock barely had to move to slide against her clit.

"I love you, Alice. I love you more than my own immortality, more than the beauty in the world, more than anything else I've ever encountered in a thousand years." Each swipe of his cock drove her higher and she rolled so she was on her stomach. He grabbed her ass and pulled her hips high to change the angle and thrust into her even deeper.

Her breath came in desperate gasps. "I love you too. So much."

Their orgasms hit faster than Alice believed possible, their moans intermingled with one another as they both went over the edge together.

Christopher leaned his forehead against hers, his breath slowly evening out. "Whatever happens, we're together."

Alice nodded. "Forever."

Christopher lay on his stomach on the castle's peaked roof and checked his watch, counting down the seconds before the explosives were set to demolish the building's entrance. Margot and her forces were harnessed up along the top of the roofline, ropes attached to the castle's stone gargoyles already hooked into the straps on their waists. They'd spooked the security cameras with looping footage to hide their position, but Christopher didn't like how exposed they were out in the open. Margot caught his eye and nodded in encouragement, her expression alight with anticipation. He wished he shared her thrill.

They'd separated their forces among Christopher's four lieutenants, each with a specific timed mission: Ben's team would infiltrate the castle's hallways and throne room ahead of the coronation to position as many UV flash bombs as possible. Danny's team was in charge of diverting as many of Rhys's forces as possible to the furthest reaches of the castle grounds, away from the power of Rhys's voice. Valerie and Margot's two teams would crash through the ancient, stained, glass windows of the throne room attacking from both sides to clear the room and get innocents out of the way before Christopher swept in to defeat Rhys. It depended on their key advantages over Rhys' forces: their trust in one another, and their ability to improvise.

This plan also positioned Alice on Ben's team, helping the inventor set up his devices to their best advantage. There was no denying Alice's expertise was needed there, but Christopher's hands shook thinking about how the only confirmation he had that she was okay were the hourly group texts with updates about the number and placements of the bombs. With every passing moment in between texts, he fought to push away the nightmares of Rhys catching her, stringing her up on his throne room wall, and making Christopher watch as he tore her to pieces. *If he has her, Rhys would damn sure let me know.* Christopher held onto that not-so-comforting thought as he steadied himself.

Three...two...one.

An explosion burning so hot its flames licked blue and white blasted open the front doors of the castle. Screams rang out from within the castle, the sound of stampeding feet thumping down the hallways as staff and guests of the coronation searched for safe exits. Christopher could almost imagine he heard Rhys's voice through the chaos screaming orders at people.

A second explosion thundered from the East side of the castle where Margot's team and Christopher waited. It was smaller than the explosion at the front gate, but the heat was intense enough Christopher could feel it against his face even seventy feet up.

The group text to all the lieutenants' phones came through at once from Alice, still hidden in the throne room: "*Half of Rhys's forces gone 2 investigate. Most guests cleared.*"

Margot didn't hesitate. She made the arranged signal with her fist and her twenty vampires and

Christopher all descended the side of the building, kicking out the stained glass windows of the throne room and bursting into the immense room.

The coronation was already underway. The main room was filled with rows of long, wooden benches and Rhys stood at the top of the room's dais wearing a sly smirk and their sire's finest regalia. A priest, who looked a lot like Rhys's barbed-wire-tattooed sireling in a hood, stood poised with his hand raised in blessing and a vacant, mind-controlled expression on his face. The crown of their vampire kingdom was still on its ceremonial pedestal, gleaming dangerously.

"This man is not your rightful king," Christopher bellowed.

The remaining coronation guests who hadn't fled all turned to watch Christopher advance down the central aisle of the throne room. Christopher recognized many of the faces, vampires who had known the royal family for centuries.

Margot's forces stood protectively in a semicircle around Christopher, keeping his path to Rhys clear. As he advanced, Ben's forces emerged from the room's alcoves to fill in gaps from the ranks. He caught a glimpse of Alice, dressed in black and armed with a sword and UV grenades strapped crossways down her torso, joining the group surrounding him. He pushed aside the worry gnawing at his insides. *If she is a casualty of this battle, I will never forgive myself.*

"Now, brother," Rhys tutted from his chair. "Jealousy is not a good color on you."

"I will not stand by and let your thirst for power destroy our people." Worried gasps sprung out among the coronation's attendees. Some were still trying to flee, but many of the older ones had stayed, curious to see how this played out.

"So dramatic, Christopher." Rhys spoke calmly. He picked up the crown from its resting place, placing the ring of gold filigree onto his head. He sat back in his throne, smiling. "I only seek to be what you can never be: a strong leader."

A click from the rafters let Christopher know the cameras Ben had installed throughout the room were switched on, broadcasting what was happening in the throne room to all the vampire television stations worldwide.

"A leader is someone who people *choose* to follow. You seek to rule solely through *hortari*, intimidation, and fear."

"You only want the throne for yourself." Rhys snarled. "You've been after our sire's power for *centuries*, always badgering him to change what makes us vampires."

Through the open windows, Christopher could hear the sounds of clashing metal and shouting. One of his teams was fighting against Rhys's goons. He sent up a quick prayer to any gods who were listening that none of them would be hurt.

"And what is it that makes us vampires, brother?" Christopher asked.

Rhys rose from the throne, standing tall with his hands above his head. "Blood and strength!"

Many of the guests roared in support, along with a sprinkling of cheers and assents from Rhys's guards around the walls.

"Yet you stand there, shedding no blood," Christopher said. "My sirelings fight for me of their own free will because they know me, they've worked with me, and they know the vision I have for our kingdom comes from a sincere desire to see us progress and grow. Can you say the same, brother?"

"You question my honorable intentions?" Rhys held his empty hands out like a saintly benediction. The crowd was lapping it up, looking between Rhys, secure on his throne, and Christopher surrounded by armed guards. Christopher knew who looked like the usurper. *This isn't going to work.*

"You can prove it." Alice had snuck closer in the cluster of guards surrounding him. Her voice was only a whisper, but it cut through the sound of blood pumping in Christopher's ears.

"No, I can't," Christopher said.

"You can." Alice pulled a dagger from her boot and sliced a cut along Christopher's arm.

He jumped back, startled and surprised that she of all people would be the one to attack him. The blood gleamed red in the candlelight of the throne room, and the smell of it tickled his nose as it wafted past. Beside him, Margot grabbed a fan from her belt, each rib edged with a razor-sharp talon, and started waving it behind him, the breeze pushing the scent of Christopher's blood across the room.

That's it.

Christopher held his bleeding arm aloft, addressing the people. "You wish to know my intentions? Here they are. The blood doesn't lie." He turned to Rhys. "If your would-be king has nothing to hide, then surely he will join me in proving so."

The crowd murmured approvingly. A few of the older vampires moved towards Christopher, bowing slightly with respect. Others too far away to smell Christopher's blood spread the word to their neighbors until the whole room was alight with speculative looks toward Rhys. Christopher's blood clearly spelled out his intentions for the throne and his people. It was an unbeatable campaign.

"You want to *cut* me? I believe that's a direct threat against your future king," Rhys growled. "How *dare* you and your rabble disrespect me in such a manner. GUARDS!" He shrieked, a shrill, echoing wail that bounced across the high ceilings of the throne room. "Kill them! Cut off their heads and bring them to me in SACKS!"

Screams rose from the remaining crowd as most of them bolted in all directions, shoving each other in an undignified attempt to get away from Rhys's soldiers.

Rhys's muscled guards couldn't resist the *hortari* in Rhys's command and ran at Christopher and his people, their arms poised overhead for neck strikes. Christopher's heart twisted for them. Many of their eyes were wide and scared. Christopher didn't want to think how many atrocities Rhys had forced them to commit since becoming vampires.

"Now!" Christopher shouted, and Ben and Margot's teams surrounding him whipped heavy cloaks and sunglasses from their packs and covered all their exposed skin.

Alice didn't hesitate. She withdrew the detonator from her sleeve and pressed the button with a magnificent glow of satisfaction on her face. Rhys's guards nearly made it to Christopher before brilliant flashes of light detonated across the room. Christopher adjusted his sunglasses, proud that Alice's calculations had been correct. There wasn't a single inch of the throne room unaffected by the UV's flashes.

Rhys and his guards screamed and grunted in the light, their skin smoking slightly as the UV rays burned their sensitive flesh. Many of those surrounding Rhys who got the worst of the blast fell to the ground unconscious.

"Get up! I command you to kill them all! As your sire, I demand it of you!" Rhys screeched from where he thrashed on the floor. "Kill them for your king!"

The guards who could still move pulled themselves from the ground like marionettes on strings. Many had expressions of complete terror frozen on their faces. Their arms chopped the air in front of them like wind-up toys, moving in spasming, wild thrusts toward Christopher and his followers.

"Spread out!" Margot bellowed, yelling the commands she and Christopher had arranged earlier so that in the heat of battle he didn't accidentally use *hortari* against his people. "Try and avoid killing them, they didn't choose this!"

The cluster of sirelings surrounding Christopher broke into smaller groups, Margot staying close to Christopher while the rest ran toward the corners of the room, breaking Rhys's men into isolated groups who Ben's team hiding in the room's rafters could shoot with paralytic-tipped arrows. They fell in swaths, Rhys's soldiers' expressions filled with relief as the arrows stopped their movements. Margot and Ben's teams on the ground immediately chained up the unmoving and unconscious guards before the shock of the UV rays or the arrows wore off.

"Get reinforcements!" Rhys bellowed, pointing to one of his guards cowering behind the throne. "Tell them I will eat their sirelings if they disobey me!" Rhys bellowed.

"Brother, think about what you're doing!" Christopher shouted. "You are only harming your own people!"

Margot was hard at work defending herself against one of Rhys's better soldiers, a six-foot tall muscled woman with a shock of bright pink hair. They moved so fast, Christopher didn't dare interfere for fear of hurting Margot. Their sparing cleared the area around them, their clashing axes sending sparks into the air.

"My people exist to serve me!" Rhys yelled.

His shout distracted Margot's opponent and Margot laughed triumphantly as she launched a flying kick through the air that sent the woman sprawling to the ground. Margot planted her knee firmly in the back of Rhys's minion as she clanked heavy manacles around the woman's wrists.

"I always wanted to use these outside of the bedroom," Margot said with a wink.

"Is this really the time for--" Christopher started to say, but was cut short by the sight of Alice across the room.

Alice stood in the middle of the battle, beautiful as she shouted orders to the team repositioning another wave of the UV flash bombs. Christopher sprinted forward to help as Alice ducked under a minion's swinging axe and continued her work undeterred. The soldier facing her couldn't have been older than twenty when he was turned, acne blotching his face for eternity.

My brother is evil.

"Stay away from her." Christopher stepped in between the boy and Alice.

"Can't, sir," the boy said through clenched teeth. "Must kill."

"You can fight it!" Alice cried, still prudently standing behind Christopher. "I broke the *hortari*, so can you."

The boy gasped, and for a second, his axe hesitated on the downswing. Christopher held his breath, hoping for a miracle, then the blade continued down and Christopher dodged out of the way, missing getting an axe dug into his shoulder by a hair.

"I'm sorry!" the boy wailed. "I can't stop it!"

Alice unhooked one of the grenades from her holster and pulled the pin, throwing it at the boy just as she raised the edge of her cloak to cover herself and Christopher. The dangerous light blazed around the corner of her cloak and the boy fell screaming, his axe skidding away. Christopher jumped forward, slapping cuffs on the boy before he could grab his weapon.

"Thank you," the boy gasped as he lay curled on the ground.

The sounds of battle outside the throne room were dimming, replaced with victorious chanting of Christopher's name. Reinforcements streamed in as Valerie's team finished securing the last door and flooded the ballroom to help take down those still-standing among Rhys's forces.

Danny's was the last team to swarm in wearing triumphant expressions.

"We tricked thirty of them into a storage container!" he yelled.

"That's great!" Christopher replied. "Why don't we--" He didn't finish when an axe sliced so close to his ear, Christopher felt the breeze of it on his cheek.

Rhys stood an arm's length away, his mouth twisted into a snarl, an axe twirling in each hand so fast they blurred in silver circles on either side of him.

"You think you've won? You're nothing!" Rhys bellowed. His arms flashed forward with deadly speed, the twin axes spinning for Christopher's neck.

"I've got a shot, I can take him down," Ben's voice yelled down from the rafters, light glinting off the tip of his arrow.

"He's mine!" Christopher called up. In a fluid motion, he withdrew a knife from his belt, diving to grab the fallen teenager's axe still at Alice's feet. Christopher circled his brother warily, looking for the twitching tell of when he was going to strike.

"Watch your words, brother," Rhys smirked. "You might actually show some balls and give an order to one of your precious sirelings." He attacked without warning in a flurry of jabs, each axe swipe perilously close to Christopher's neck.

Christopher blocked and dodged, knowing that when it came to hand to hand combat, his brother was always willing to cheat.

Unless..."Do you hear the cameras rolling, brother?" Christopher ducked just before one of the axes connected with his head and he rolled through Rhys's wide stance. "Everyone will know what happened here."

"What are you talking about?"

Christopher sprung to his feet, kicking Rhys hard in the back, surprising his brother and knocking him off balance. "You're a greedy liar who uses *hortari* to treat your sirelings as cannon fodder."

Rhys dodged out of the way, rolling under Christopher's swing with his awes twirling. "I *saved* them. You have no idea how broken these people were when I found them, how much they regretted the choices they'd made." He feinted to the right with one axe, the left striking out so fast Christopher couldn't duck away quick enough. The axe's fine edge sliced a long cut down Christopher's forearm, dripping blood.

"I gave them *immortality*," Rhys yelled. "And then I took away their burden of choice."

"They're *killing* people." Christopher flexed his injured arm. The cut burned and would need stitches, but adrenaline made it easy to shake off.

Rhys rolled his eyes. "You just don't get it. They *want* this. They're free from consequences. They're just following orders. No guilt. No repercussions."

"Then you've promised them an illusion." Christopher advanced on his brother, his axe and knife flying in a complex sequence of swings and stabs which had Rhys retreating backward to dodge out of the way. "Everything we do has consequences." He swung his knife for Rhys's stomach as he kicked out for Rhys's knees. Rhys jumped away, but for the first time, he showed fear. "Everything else is just excuses."

Distantly he heard their audience murmuring to themselves, nodding heads of agreement and tones of consideration surround them.

Christopher smiled. "The entire kingdom sees you for what you are."

"I am a *king*! I'm the savior of our people!"

"You're a weak, terrified coward."

Rhys screamed in mindless fury, swinging his axe in a wild arc. Christopher raised one arm, blocking the down-swing of Rhys's axe on his metal arm-guard while he leapt in a roundhouse kick, connecting with Rhys's head.

The sound of Rhys's body hitting the ground was the most satisfying thud Christopher had heard in ages. Christopher snapped cuffs on his brother's hands and stepped back. Rhys lay sprawled across the red carpet like a broken doll.

"Long live the vampire king," Margot's impressed voice rang out uncomfortably loud in the now-silent throne room.

"Is that it?" Danny asked from his perch atop a guard's back.

"We did it!" Alice ran to Christopher, wrapping her arms around his neck. She stood on tiptoe and brought her lips to his.

He smiled against Alice's lips as he pressed into her, his tongue roaming her mouth with the same ferocity his hands roamed her body.

"Let's go take the former-prince and the other prisoners to the dungeon." Margot shouted across the hall with a laugh. "Our new king is busy making out."

Alice decided she liked sitting on a throne. The throne room was absolutely stunning now that Margot had insisted on redecorating. Alice never thought she'd ever feel so at home. Ruling had taken a few months to get used to, especially as Christopher and his sire line were busy writing new policies, ferreting out Rhys's remaining supporters, and building up new allies to solidify their rule. It still boggled Alice's mind that when Christopher talked about his rule, he meant *centuries*. There were moments when she still couldn't quite believe only a few months ago she'd been a photographer whose most ambitious dream was to financially support herself with her art. Now she was the acting *Queen of the Vampires*. Submitting her resignation letter at her old day job had been nearly as satisfying as helping defeat Rhys.

A group of vampires knelt below her in the throne room, heads bowed. A female vampire who looked like she was in her mid-twenties, but was probably older than Alice's great-grandmother, stepped forward. She made a small cut on her finger, raising the blood toward Alice. Since Alice's impromptu move during the coronation that betrayed Rhys's malicious intentions, small gestures of bloodletting when making a request to the court had become standard practice.

"We have come to make a formal petition to the court to break our *hortari*." The woman's blood stank of terror, long-held grudges, and a spirit nearly broken to pieces. The others huddled behind the leader made small cuts as well. *All women*, Alice noticed, with a sense of unease. Since it was known that Alice wasn't bound to Christopher any more, vampire women coming forward and asking her to break their own bonds was distressingly common.

"Unfortunately, the *hortari* isn't something that I or anyone else has the power to lift," Alice said. "I broke mine because I was desperate to save the people I loved. With sufficient will and training, you can do the same."

"Please, *teach us*," the woman in front said. "Our sire is a sadistic bastard. We were only able to get away by tricking and gagging him. We must break our bond to him before he finds us." The others behind her nodded.

A sinking feeling filled Alice's chest. There was so much still to do, so much left to fix. Having no accountability for sires for so long had kept so many awful practices in the dark. Regulating how sires treated their sirelings was the first step towards trying to make things right. *It's a good thing we have time.*

"You have sanctuary here for as long as you need," Alice said. "And I will teach you as best I can." She beckoned to one of the stewards to take them to the wing they were refurnishing specifically for guests.

"Take them to clean rooms and collect statements about their sire and who else might still be under his thrall. We'll send out Danny to lead a team to question and detain the sire."

Alice kept an expression of royal serenity on her face until the last woman left the room, then sunk against the back of the door.

"That was well done," Margot said, approaching from the side of the room where she'd been watching the proceedings.

Alice rubbed her forehead. "I still don't know why it's me who has to do this. I'm not the one who fought my evil brother in order to become the ruler." *An evil brother pouting in the dungeon for at least the next millennia*, Alice thought. It was only Christopher's belief that Rhys could someday change that had stayed his execution for treason.

Margot gave Alice a pat on the shoulder that would have been heavy enough to bruise if Alice had still been human.

"You're a natural. And you're learning the rest. Christopher is out getting to know the people and enforcing the rules, which only he has the centuries of experience to do. And you're new to being a vampire, so you don't have all the baggage that the rest of us carry."

"I guess." Alice looked at Margot and saw a wealth of understanding in the woman's brown eyes. "I just miss him."

"Anyone who told you that ruling a scattered nation of blood-sucking immortals was going to be easy was having you on."

"Haha. Funny."

"And I happen to know that a certain king arrived a few minutes ago through the side entrance and might be hogging up the hot water to make himself look presentable for his queen."

"Christopher is home?" Alice jumped off the throne and started to run toward the stairs before turning back around to look at Margot. "Why didn't you say something earlier?"

Margot grinned. "It's my prerogative as your Princess of Intelligence. I get to decide when and how you know things. Trust me, you wanted to give him a few minutes to wash off before you saw him."

"You're the *Head* of Intelligence," Alice said, confused.

"Yes, and my sire is king, so I'm a princess." Margot waved a hand at Alice, effectively dismissing her.

Alice didn't bother to chastise her. Margot was usually right. And Christopher was waiting.

Alice raced up the stairs, memories of the first time Christopher and she raced to the bedroom as vampires flashing through her mind, warming her insides. She kicked open their bedroom door.

Christopher stood in the middle of the room wearing only a towel. His smile when he turned to face her was radiant. He held out her arms, the towel fell, and Alice jumped into his arms with so much enthusiasm, her crown fell off her head and rolled under the bed.

His kiss devoured her, as passionate as the first time he ever held her. He murmured into her mouth. "You look beautiful, your majesty. Are you wearing anything too precious to tear off of you right now? Because I really need you naked."

"Hmm, go slow, I want to savor this." Her hands slid across his skin, still slightly wet from his shower. "You look far too sexy to be king." She gripped his bare ass, amazed again that she'd somehow ended up with the perfect man. "Are you sure you're not some roguish, activist prince trying to change the world?"

"That was last year. What did you tell me the first time we met? Even those frozen in time can get redefined by context."

She laughed. "That doesn't sound like me."

He kissed her soundly as he unzipped the back of her dress, caressing along her spine. "It sounds eloquent, so it sounds *exactly* like you." His hands against the cool skin of her back felt divine.

Alice leaned back to look at her face. "I love you more than anything in this world, Christopher."

His hands paused. "There's something I've been meaning to talk to you about, Alice."

"Oh? Does this mean I have to stop getting undressed?" She pushed down the spray of nerves that jingled in her stomach.

He chuckled. "Heavens, no. Are you mad, woman? I would never stop you from getting undressed." As he spoke, he helped pull down her dress, unclasping her bra, and standing in awe for a long moment at her naked breasts. He walked her to the bed and lifted her up, sitting beside her with a grave expression on his face as he played one of her nipples into an erect point.

"Alice," he breathed the word like a prayer, leaning over to latch his mouth around her breast as his fingers traced lines down her stomach to cup her mound. She arched her back into the exquisiteness of his touch, grabbing his hair to pull him closer. "You've been acting as queen in my stead for months now, but you've been the queen of my heart since we met." He lifted his mouth from her nipple to capture her mouth. "Please, make me the happiest being in all of time and space by agreeing to be my queen, my wife, in truth. Marry me."

Joy erupted through Alice's chest and up through her head in a rush. She rolled on top of Christopher's naked body, latching onto his mouth and then moving to his neck.

"I broke the *hortari* to be with you." She licked the musky sweat from his skin, savoring everything about her perfect king. "I want you as my husband."

He tilted his neck, baring his throat to her elongating teeth. "Then take me. Take me, my love." At his words, she sunk her teeth into his flesh, drinking deep. Christopher's essence flowed through her as she sucked his blood: his joy her joy, his love her love. His cock slid into her warmth as they moved together. She gasped with happiness as he bit deep into her shoulder, their feelings combined as they drank and rode each other in waves of pleasure that built like oncoming storms.

They came together, Alice feeling like she was floating on their shared ecstasy. She lay panting against his chest. Out there in the world, there would be many battles left to face. Injustice didn't end with the installation of one just monarch. Years of work lay ahead, as well as moments of wonder and awe and captured moments.

Her hand found the camera beside the bed and she snapped a picture of Christopher's sleeping face. She glanced at the frozen image in the viewfinder and sighed with contentment. Perhaps the context of the picture would change over time, but one thing would never change: she loved Christopher, and would love Christopher, for as long as immortality allowed.

Dear Reader,

We hoped you enjoyed **The Vampire's Throne**. We really love this world and creating more places and people to inhabit it. Many readers wrote asking; "What's up with Lola?" Well, stay tuned for more of Lola's mysterious meddling because the adventures at AUDREY'S (and the paranormal romantic interludes) aren't over.

When we first published this series, we got a lot of emails from fans thanking us for these books. Some liked certain series and sets of characters more than others. As authors, we love feedback. Your appreciation for this world is the reason why we keep writing books around AUDREY'S and Lola.

Reviews are increasingly tough to come by these days. You, the reader, have the power now to make or break a book.

So, tell us what you like, what you loved, even what you hated. We'd love to hear from you. You can write us at a.j.tipton.author@gmail.com, or visit our website at https://ajtiptonauthor.wordpress.com. We can also connect through our e-mail subscription list, Facebook, and Twitter.

Thank you so much for reading **The Vampire's Throne** and for spending time with our wacky brains.

Have fun, everybody

Annie & Jess ("AJ") Tipton

Meet AJ Tipton

AJ Tipton is the pseudonym of a writing team: Annie and Jess (Get it? "AJ." You get it). Corporate drones by day, we spend our evenings writing fantasies to astound, arouse, and amuse. Located in Brooklyn, we are total dorks and love it.

Want more stories of the bizarre and wondrous? Sign up for the new publications subscription list and you'll be the first to know when new books become available. There might also be other surprises along the way. Or just contact us directly at a.j.tipton.author@gmail.com

Our ideas for future books--everything from sex robots to ghost brothels--will keep us busy for many years to come, so follow along for the fun and let us know what series you like best. We love to hear from readers.

Facebook: https://www.facebook.com/AJTiptonAuthor

Twitter: https://twitter.com/AJTiptonAuthor

Blog: https://ajtiptonauthor.wordpress.com/

Made in the USA
Las Vegas, NV
18 December 2020

13607764R00081